THE OTHER MRS. WATSON'S CASEBOOK

The indomitable Amelia Watson, second wife of the famous doctor, continues to bend her formidable intellect to solving further crimes. Whether foiling anarchists, investigating a possible murder committed high above the streets of London, rescuing her old theatre colleague Harry Benbow from a decidedly awkward scrape involving a haunted house, untangling the connection behind a trail of all-too-real headless corpses, or determining the truth behind a case of apparent spontaneous combustion, this respect-able Edwardian lady remains a force to be reckoned with.

MICHAEL MALLORY

THE OTHER MRS. WATSON'S CASEBOOK

Complete and Unabridged

LINFORD
Leicester

First published in Great Britain

First Linford Edition
published 2017

A catalogue record for this book is available
from the British Library.

ISBN 978–1–4448–3383–6

Published by
F. A. Thorpe (Publishing)
Anstey, Leicestershire

Set by Words & Graphics Ltd.
Anstey, Leicestershire
Printed and bound in Great Britain by
T. J. International Ltd., Padstow, Cornwall

This book is printed on acid-free paper

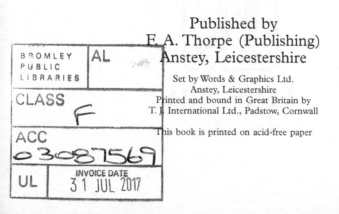

The Adventure of the Tangled Web

'John, I would like to speak with you,' I said tensely, glancing askance at the long, thin Buddha who was draped across the sofa in our day room. His eyes closed, his bony hands tented together on the chest, Mr. Sherlock Holmes was to all appearances dead, save for the wisps of noxious cigarette smoke that emanated, dragon-like, from his nostrils. 'Now, please, dear.'

I marched my husband — who happened to be Mr. Holmes' greatest, if not only, friend — to our bedroom, and shut the door behind us. Before I could begin, John held his hands up and stated: 'I know what you are going to say, Amelia. I realise it has been difficult for you having Holmes stay with us.'

'No, John, spending one's childhood in

1

a workhouse is *difficult*. This is *impossible*!'

'But there was nowhere else he could go! Mrs. Hudson has already let out 22lb to someone else, and I cannot simply pack him off to a hotel.'

'Why not?'

John sighed heavily. 'Because I must keep watch over him. I have done too well in informing the world that Holmes is retired, so no one is bringing him cases. He has come back to complete inactivity and boredom, and in such periods he becomes morose. Amelia, if I am not around to prevent him, he will surely take to the needle again.'

Faintly, I heard our front door open and listened to the footsteps of Missy, our maid, whom our house guest had sent out to fetch a copy of *The Illustrated London News*. 'I understand your concern, darling,' I continued, sympathetically, 'but we must do something! He has not only usurped Missy's bedroom but he has turned her into his personal servant, running errands for him at all times of the day or night. And those cigarettes! Until recently, John, I was not aware that seaweed burned.'

I was about to continue airing my grievances but was interrupted by a cry of 'Watson!' coming from the day room. As though by reflex, John dashed out to see what the trouble was, and I followed. We found our guest clutching the newspaper and looking stricken.

'Have you seen this?' he shouted. 'St. James's Hall is about to be demolished to make room for a new hotel. My entire past is being eradicated one building at a time.' I remembered John having spoken of Mr. Holmes' fondness for attending concerts at St. James's, though his reaction to the news seemed a bit extreme. He sank back as though wounded and dropped the newspaper, which John retrieved and began to read.

'What about this, Holmes?' he said. 'It says here: 'In cordoning off access to Swallow Street, which is to remain closed throughout the demolition, police noticed that the walls of the Hall had been recently damaged as though by explosives.' This sounds like something that could be worth investigating.'

'And what would I uncover?' Mr. Holmes moaned. 'A group of young vandals using the walls of a doomed building to play with fire. Bring me a real crime, Watson, before my mind dies of starvation.'

'I am sorry, Holmes,' John said, gently, 'but you know as well as I that the chance of someone simply showing up at our doorstep with a knotty problem is remote, to say the least.'

'Then you should cultivate more interesting acquaintances,' the detective snapped, closing his eyes and waving us away. John looked to me with an expression of exasperation and strode off, and I was very grateful that neither of them could deduce what I was at that moment thinking.

However, never let it be said that I am not a charitable person. I endured the doleful detective for the rest of the day with a smile, albeit a clenched one. Even though I went out for a couple of hours during the afternoon (unfortunately leaving poor Missy to contend with

Mr. Holmes on her own), upon my return I did my best to engage him in diversionary conversation in an attempt to raise him out of his black mood. That I failed to do so was hardly my fault.

The following day saw no change in his demeanour. If anything, he was more gloomy and waspish, at least until a little after two o'clock in the afternoon, when there came a knock on our door. Since Missy was out fetching more of those loathsome cigarettes Mr. Holmes had become addicted to, I answered it and was startled to see a small, bespectacled, red-faced man with greying hair and a purple-tinged carnation in his lapel. He tapped his fingers nervously on a leather satchel.

'Pardon me, madam,' he said in a thin, reedy voice, 'but I was told by Dr. John H. Watson, with whom I consulted this morning about a recurring pain in the region of my lower back, that Mr. Sherlock Holmes was here. I happened to mention to the doctor that I had recently experienced a very curious occurrence, and he suggested that I seek

Mr. Holmes' advice.'

Before I could say a word, Mr. Holmes' voice called out: 'Show him in, Mrs. Watson.'

Against my better judgment I escorted the small man into the day room and offered him a chair. Mr. Holmes, meanwhile, remained sprawled on the sofa as though he had been tossed there, though his eyes were now open and clear. 'I am so sorry that you have suffered a reversal of fortunes through unemployment,' he told the man, 'though I trust your room in the boarding house near Covent Garden remains affordable to you.'

The little man's mouth dropped open.

'Your expression tells me my deductions are correct,' Holmes replied, sitting up straight, 'but of course they would be. Your suit is quite out of fashion, indicating that you do not have the finances to purchase a new one. You carry the satchel of a clerk, yet there is no ink stain on the middle finger of either hand, ergo you have not recently been employed. The wilt of your carnation boutonniere implies it is at least a day

6

old, and therefore acquired from a
discard box behind a flower stand at
Covent Garden, which is the only place I
am aware of in London to obtain a flower
of that particular colour. Your financial
situation combined with the absence of a
wedding ring strongly suggest that you
are living in a boarding house. The traces
of horse residue on your shoes tell me
that you habitually walk rather than pay
for public transportation, but since the
pain you described in your lower back
would prevent most people from taking
an unnecessary walk, such as a trip to
Covent Garden for flowers, I must
conclude that the Garden is comfortably
close to your home. Now then, how may I
be of service to you, Mr . . . ?'

'Grinney, sir, Lester Grinney,' the man
said. 'It seems, Mr. Holmes, that someone
has broken into my rooms.'

'A matter for the Metropolitan force, I
should think.'

'Ordinarily I would agree, but there
was something peculiar about this break-
in. You see, Mr. Holmes, nothing was
removed from my rooms, but something

was left behind.' Opening his satchel, the little man withdrew an object roughly the size of a pocket watch, wrapped in a cloth. Laying it down on the floor, he carefully unfolded it. Inside was an ornament made of what looked like gold and black onyx, carved in the shape of a beetle. 'I found it next to me in bed when I woke up that morning,' he went on. 'Later, I discovered my door had been forced open. Do you know what it is or what it means?'

Mr. Holmes picked up the strange object and examined it. 'It is an Egyptian scarab of the Ptolemaic period, I should think,' he answered. 'As to what it means, Mr. Grinney, I can answer in one word: danger. There are deadly cults in the world who deliver such objects as warnings to those they feel have wronged them. This is a perilous business, Mr. Grinney, and my advice to you is to be careful. Your life may be in grave danger. I trust you will not mind if I keep this scarab for the time being?'

'No, not at all, but — '

'Thank you. Return to your rooms,

take no chances, speak to no one, and come to see me again in two days. I may have an answer for you then. Good day, Mr. Grinney. Please show him out, Mrs. Watson.'

The speed with which Mr. Holmes dismissed the little man quite startled me, though I did as requested. After seeing him out I returned to the day room to see the detective peering through the window. 'What did you make of that fellow?' he asked.

'Well, he appeared rather nervous,' I replied.

'Indeed. Only the most skilful of liars can hide their nervousness, and our man was less than skilful.'

'Then you don't believe — '

'That ridiculous story supported by this costume jewellery scarab? Of course not!' He turned away from the window, eyes flashing. 'The man was a complete fraud. Consider how much unsolicited information he provided, the hallmark of a prevaricator. I doubt your husband has ever seen this man, let alone treated him, though I could not rid myself of the notion that I had seen him before.'

'But if John did not tell him to come here, how did he know where to find you?'

'Ah, how indeed!' Mr. Holmes cried, dashing into Missy's — currently his — room, and ransacking the clothing that lay about in heaps. 'Obviously, word has got out among the criminal class that I am back in London, so having learned of my whereabouts, they decided to send our Mr. Grinney along to distract me.'

'Distract you from what?'

'From whatever crime they are really planning,' he said, tossing shirts and stockings to and fro. 'Stupidly, they thought they could wave a stage prop and a penny dreadful plot in front of me and I would take the bait. And by pretending to do exactly that, I have lured them into complacency, leaving them completely unaware that the subject of my interest is not this ridiculous bauble, but Grinney himself.'

'What could be your interest in Mr. Grinney?' I asked, breathlessly.

'Who he is, who he works for, and the

conspiracy of which he is a part. I intend to follow him and discover the truth regarding all three.'

'In that case, shouldn't you have already left?' I asked.

'I will have no difficulty finding him. We know he lives near Covent Garden, and his short height should make him easy to identify. And unless I miss my guess, he will dine this evening at a fish-and-chip stand near the Garden.'

'How could you possibly know that?'

'Really, Mrs. Watson, could you not detect the scent of malt vinegar on the kerchief that the man had wrapped the scarab in?' he replied. 'That, coupled with the grease stains, indicated that fish and chips is our friend's favourite dish. Rest assured, madam, I will find him. Now then, I shall need a few things before I set out. Might I borrow your maid for the rest of the afternoon?'

Upon hearing Missy return from her errand, I instructed her to assist Mr. Holmes in his requests, no matter how bizarre they might seem, then made my own excuses to leave. Quickly gathering my things, I pinned on a hat and practically ran out onto the street. Hailing the first hansom I saw, I climbed in and promised the driver a tip if he could get me to Maiden Lane within ten minutes. As we sped along, I repeated in my mind the wisdom of Sir Walter Scott: *Oh, what a tangled web we weave. When first we practise to deceive!* Why had I not left well enough alone?

The driver earned his extra tuppence by delivering me to a small house on Maiden Lane in exactly nine minutes. I dashed inside the building and headed straight for the door marked 'A' — a room I had visited the previous day. Rapidly knocking, I said, 'Harry, it's Amelia. If you're in there, open up!'

The door quickly opened and I was greeted by my long-time friend, and long-ago colleague in amateur theatrics, Harry Benbow — alias Lester Grinney. He had removed the spectacles and cleansed the ruddiness from his face, though the artificial grey remained in his hair. 'Amelia, I didn't expect to see you here so soon,' he said, his natural South

London speech replacing the highborn accent of Lester Grinney.

'Harry, what happened to the plan?' I demanded, closing his door of his impoverished room. 'I thought we agreed that a friend of yours would be the one to visit Mr. Holmes, not you!'

'Well, me chum Bobbie couldn't do it after all, so I decided to give her a go myself, though I don't mind telling you, I nearly dropped my onions when Mr. Holmes started reading me like the *Police Gazette*, right down to where I lived. But what did you think of my performance, ducks?'

'It was fine, Harry, but what if Mr. Holmes had recognised you?' Harry and the detective had encountered each other once before in a case involving robbery, murder and the kinema.

'But he didn't.'

'Not yet, though at this moment he is on his way over to try and find you. He saw through your story and now he thinks you're part of some heinous crime conspiracy. Oh, what a mess I have made of things! All I wanted to do was get Mr.

Holmes away from our house for a few days before I went insane. I thought bringing him a case, even a fictional one, would be the way to do it, but all I've done is endanger you. Maybe you should hide in a hotel for a few days.'

'Gor, I can't afford that,' he said. 'I'm doing my best to keep body and soul here. Busking ain't what it used to be.'

'But you cannot stay here, Harry, Mr. Holmes will find you. Let's take a cab ride and maybe I can arrive at some solution while we travel.'

Donning a dented bowler, which he nevertheless wore with pride, Harry accompanied me to the street, where I raised my hand to hail a cab that had pulled up on the opposite kerb — at least until I saw the person who got out: a stooped, thin figure artfully wearing a broad-brimmed hat to cover short hair, and a blue velveteen dress. *My* blue velveteen dress! 'Oh, *no!*' I whispered. '*He* is here!' Grabbing Harry by the arm, I marched back into the building. But before we could disappear once more into his room, a heavy voice behind us commanded: 'What's all this then, Mr. Benbow?'

We turned to see a very broad, very bald man whose face was creased and reddened from drink, and whose hammer-like hands fidgeted nervously. 'You know the rules, Benbow, no birds in the room. There's other houses for that sort of thing.'

I am rarely rendered speechless, but this egg-domed brute's utter coarseness rendered me so. Fortunately, Harry was not. 'Bird, Mr. Stigg?' he said, professing shock, 'I will have you know that this ain't no bird, this is my sister, Amelia, come for a visit. Amelia dear, this is Mr. Stigg, owner of this pile.'

'How do you do,' I managed to say, holding a ladylike hand out to the landlord, all the while feeling my tangled web constricting around my throat.

'Right,' he replied, but instead of taking my hand, began to wipe his on his trousers. 'Sorry, got cleaning fluid on my hands. So, how long you going to be here, *sister*?'

While I did not like the tone of his voice, I strove to keep mine even. 'Not long at all,' I said, 'a quick stop before going to tea.'

'Tea, is it?' Mr. Stigg said. 'At an eating house that favours respectable ladies?'

'Of course,' I snapped.

'I'm delighted to hear it,' he said, smiling to reveal yellow stump-like teeth. 'That means one of you is in the chips, so I will be paid for the money owed on the room.' As poor Harry stood gaping, the landlord added: 'I expect payment in full by this Friday, Benbow.' Then he turned and lumbered up the hall stairway.

'That tears it,' Harry groaned. 'I might as well start packing my trunk now.'

'Pack later, Harry,' I said, 'right now we have to find a way to get you out of here.' That, however, was not to be, since at that moment there came an insistent rapping on the front door, and I had a terrifying feeling I knew who it was. 'Into your room,' I said, and once inside, I cautiously stepped to the small window that looked out onto the street. I recognised the caller immediately. 'It's Mr. Holmes, Harry,' I whispered, stepping away. 'No doubt he is checking with

16

every rooming house around Covent Garden!'

Listening at the door, I could hear the rough approach of Mr. Stigg followed by the door opening, and then Mr. Holmes' voice asking about a tenant named Lester Grinney. 'Don't know any Lester Grinney,' Mr. Stigg growled, but instead of dropping the matter and carrying on his search elsewhere, the detective kept pressing, describing his quarry and claiming that it was a matter of importance that he be found. 'I would hate to be forced to ask a constable to accompany me back here to continue my search,' Mr. Holmes concluded.

The effect the word *constable* had on Mr. Stigg was startling. 'Bl–dy hell!' he cried. 'It's no peeler's business what goes on in his house, and it's none of yours!'

The next sounds were hard to interpret, but they included a cry, followed by what sounded like a falling body. 'Bl–dy hell!' Mr. Stigg shouted again. 'Get out of here! Go on, you, get out, or I'll call a peeler meself!'

'Do so,' I heard Mr. Holmes say calmly.

'I shall be not hesitate to tell him that you raised your hand first, while I merely defended myself.'

I am afraid I cannot repeat in good conscience what the landlord said next, but I heard the front door slam. Sneaking back to the window, I peeked through and watched Mr. Holmes leap into a waiting hansom, which broke away from the kerb. 'He's gone,' I said, nearly collapsing. I turned to Harry, or at least to the spot where I had last seen Harry. Scanning the room, I found no trace of him. He had disappeared completely! 'Harry, where are you?' I called.

'Right behind you,' he answered, startling me. I whipped around and saw him grinning, having reappeared seemingly by magic.

'Have you now added invisibility to your list of talents?' I asked.

'No, but watch this,' he said, stepping back to a battered coat rack, upon which hung an equally battered greatcoat. By slipping his arms into the coat and balancing his feet on the base of the rack, he disappeared completely into the coat, leaving no trace! Popping his head out, he said, 'I used that trick once when old Stigg came 'round looking for his rent. So you go on home, ducks, and if anyone knocks on the door, I'll just disappear again.'

Had I not witnessed this bit of legerdemain, I might not have been so inclined to leave him there. But Harry was right, I had to return home.

Upon arriving there I found Mr. Holmes in our day room, speaking on the telephone. Draped across the back of a chair was a shirt with a dark smudge on it, which I instinctively inspected.

'Pray, do not touch that!' Mr. Holmes snapped, and I raised my hands in alarm. Seconds later he concluded his telephone conversation and rang off. 'Things are becoming clearer, Mrs. Watson,' he said. 'I have been conversing with my brother Mycroft and now I understand our little man's game all too clearly.'

'With *Mycroft*?' I blurted, trying not to show too much alarm. I knew from experience that Mycroft Holmes, who presented himself as a simple, sedentary civil servant, was really a powerful, if secretive, force within Whitehall. How much more trouble could I land Harry in?

That evening I retired to bed early, in order to worry in comfort. The next morning I awoke with an aching head and a new sense of concern, as John informed me that Mr. Holmes had been up and out early, on some new mission of dire importance. 'You should have seen him, Amelia,' he said, beaming, 'it was like the old Holmes had returned.'

'How wonderful,' I groaned.

After John had left for his surgery, I invited Missy to sit with me, as she was as nearly exhausted as I was from her tenure as servant to Sherlock Holmes. The two of us had barely had a chance to settle ourselves when an insistent knock was at the door. '*Now* what?' I demanded, and Missy instinctively started to rise. 'No, dear, you rest,' I told her. 'I shall get it.' Throwing the door open, I encountered the wide-eyed, perspiring Harry Benbow, who rushed in, tightly clutching his battered satchel.

'My head's in the noose now, Amelia!' he cried. 'Your friend Sherlock Holmes was snooping around my place this morning with a couple o' coppers, and my guess is they were looking for these.' He opened the satchel and withdrew a fist-sized black object with a fuse. It was a bomb, the sight of which forced Missy to retreat to her room in terror. 'And get an eyeful o' this,' Harry went on, withdrawing a sheet of paper upon which rows of meaningless letters and numbers had been jotted, around a makeshift map. Examining it, I read: *Fr PM Vc to Bres — BP 5/19–11a.*

'Where did you get these things, Harry?'

'Late last night I heard a tap-tap-tap on the door and Stigg's voice calling out, 'Mr. Benbow, are you there?' I figure he wants his bread-and-honey, so I go into my disappearing routine. But once he figures I ain't home, instead of going away, he unlocks the door and comes in! He looks around then tucks some stuff under my bed and hightails it out. Naturally, I take a peep at what he hid and I see it's a ruddy bomb! But it ain't lit, so I know he's not trying to blow me to Kingdom Come. So I ask myself, what *is* he up to then? And 'fore you can say Bob's your uncle, it comes to me: he's planting some kind of evidence in my room! Well, I stash the stuff and wait till morning, and that's when your chum Sherlock Holmes shows up at the house. Quick as I could, I grabbed it all up, snuck out the front door and ran all the way here. But now I'm clean out o' ideas.'

'We must go to the Yard,' I told him, 'I'll explain it to Inspector Laurie and he will help us.' My head was beginning to throb and as I massaged it, I glanced down at the cryptic letters on the note. 'Harry, the notation *BP* on this paper, what does that suggest to you?'

'I don't know — British Patriot?'

'Or Buckingham Palace. And this, *Vc to Bres*, that might mean Victoria Street to Bressenden Place, the southern access route to the Palace grounds.'

'By the mews, right,' Harry said. 'So *PM* might mean Palace Mews.'

'Possibly, but more likely Prime Minister. But what is *Fr?*' In unison, Harry and I said *French.* I was beginning to feel chilled by the message that was forming from the cryptic note. 'That must have been the information that Mr. Holmes had gleaned from his brother, that the French Prime Minister was paying a visit to London. And this note, along with these bombs, can only mean — '

'Gor, he's the target!' Harry cried. 'They're gonna chuck a bomb at him on his way to the palace!'

'I hate to tell you this, Harry, but it appears your landlord is an anarchist. He's planning to assassinate the French Prime Minister and he planted these in your room to divert suspicion from himself and implicate you! And look at these numbers, *5/19 — 11a.* That can only mean May 19th — today — at eleven o'clock in the morning. Less than thirty minutes from now! I do not know if we can prevent this, Harry, but we must try!'

I gingerly gathered up the bombs and the note and shoved them back in the satchel, then hid it in the back of my wardrobe, after which I grabbed Harry by the arm and ran out to the street. Hailing the first cab that would stop, we jumped in and instructed the driver to take us to the Royal Mews. By the time we arrived — with ten minutes to spare, according to Harry's ancient watch — I was a bundle of jangled nerves. Not surprisingly, Buckingham Palace Road was closed off, and a small army of constables were stationed every couple of yards. A small crowd of people, having been alerted that something was going to take place, had also begun to form, and I instructed Harry to look for Mr. Stigg.

We milled through the crowd, trying to look inconspicuous, but always conscious of the number of police who were present. As each minute ticked away, I became more and more nervous, until . . . *'There!'* I cried, spotting the boulder head of the landlord, a distance up in the crowd. His eyes darted nervously around and at one point I saw him nod to another man, no doubt a confederate, who responded in kind. At that moment a great murmur arose from the crowd, and through the heads I saw a magnificent, ornate coach, pulled by four liveried, prancing horses, making its way up Buckingham Palace Road. 'The Prime Minister's coach!' I shouted to Harry. 'We must hurry!'

The two of us elbowed and shoved our way through the crowd, trying to get towards Stigg, who was watching the coach intently. I saw him nod again to his confederate, then reach into his pocket. 'Harry,' I cried, 'we're not going to make it!'

'Oh yes we are,' he said, then in a voice trained to reach the back row of the largest music hall in the Realm, he shouted: '*That man has a bomb!*', parting the crowd as effectively as Moses clove the Red Sea and making Mr. Stigg the focus of attention of every set of eyes. A man leapt to the street from the French Royal Coach, and seeing through the governmental dress, hat and pointed beard, I recognised him as Sherlock Holmes. He ordered the driver of the coach to speed away as four constables suddenly grabbed Mr. Stigg and wrestled him to the ground. Three other men in the crowd tried to run, but they did not get far. 'Thank God,' I sighed. But then I heard Mr. Holmes' voice shout, 'Him, too, the short one!' and within a second, Harry had been tackled by a constable and was being held!

Racing to his side, I cried, 'No, let him go!'

To say that Mr. Holmes was startled by my presence was an understatement. 'You appear to be everywhere, madam,' he pronounced, warily.

'He is not one of the criminals,' I said.

'That's right,' Harry agreed, affecting a deep, rumbling voice that I had not heard before, 'and if you will kindly release me, I will introduce myself.'

Having ascertained that Harry was unarmed, the constables released him. Massaging the small of his back (that part of his Grinney characterisation, apparently, had not been fabricated), Harry thrust out his chest and marched towards the detective. 'Like you, sir, I am a private detective. The name's Horace Bentley.'

Oh Lord! I thought, once more feeling

trapped in the tangled web.

'I had been following this here Stigg for some time, convinced he was the ringleader of a group of these Antichrists.'

Anarchists, Harry! I thought, as loudly as I could.

'I even rented a room from him so as to watch him,' he went on, 'but he began to suspect me, so I came to you for help, Mr. Holmes.'

'Posing as a client?' Holmes asked.

'Just so,' Harry agreed, 'because . . . uh . . . I desperately needed your help, and that was the best way I could think of to get you interested immediately. I talked it over with Mrs. Watson, and she agreed that this would be the best way to proceed.'

'Indeed,' Mr. Holmes said, glancing in my direction.

'Yes sir,' Harry went on. 'And I have to say, Mr. Holmes, that you lived up to your reputation. You figured out the plot without my telling you.'

'It was elementary,' the detective replied, as Stigg and his co-conspirators were being loaded into a police wagon.

'When I met with our friend Stigg yesterday and noticed that his hands were covered with black powder, the kind anarchists use in making explosives, I went so far as to contrive a physical altercation with him so that his hand-prints would leave incriminating traces of it on the clothing I was wearing, should the police require such evidence. Then I remembered reading a newspaper story about marks being found on the walls of St James's Hall, which implied that somebody had been using a vacant, soon to be demolished building to practise throwing their bombs. When I deduced that an important figure might be in danger, I notified a government official, who informed me of the French Prime Minister's impending appearance at the Palace. A visit to Stigg's rooms this morning produced even more evidence of the conspiracy. I hope that satisfies your curiosity. Now then, Mr. Bentley, I have a few questions I would like to ask you.'

'And I would love to answer them for you, Mr. Holmes, but I must be off,' Harry said, fading back into the crowd.

'Perhaps we can get together sometime.' He doffed his hat and, in a second, was gone.

Mr. Holmes then turned to me. 'I would also like to speak with you regarding your involvement in this, Mrs. Watson.'

'Certainly, Mr. Holmes,' I said. 'This evening, perhaps.' I likewise began weaving my way through the throng of people until I had left the commotion at the Palace grounds behind.

The evening was several hours away. I prayed it would be enough time for me to spin a new, hopefully satisfying web.

The Adventure of the
Two Mrs. MacGregors

'Amelia, if this is not the most singularly exhilarating experience I have ever had in my entire fifty-two years on earth, then I will be hanged!' my husband enthused. I wished I could have shared his enthusiasm, but *exhilarating* was not the word that immediately came to mind when describing being suspended some two-thousand feet in the air with nothing but a layer of reinforced wicker between my feet and the ground far, far below.

The hot air balloon in which John, myself and our pilot — an acquaintance of John's named Jack Tyson — were riding suffered another sudden buffet from the wind, and what was left of my stomach rose even higher in my throat. How John had managed to convince me to accompany him on this insane voyage of terror in honour of his birthday, I shall never know!

'Let me take her down a bit and see if we can't avoid that turbulence,' Mr. Tyson said, tugging on the rope that controlled a valve on the balloon, which hissed mightily as it expelled a quantity of gas. With my hands clenched so tightly around the support ropes that my palms chafed, I kept my gaze focused straight ahead, not because I particularly appreciated the distant, map-like view of the City, but because my neck had been frozen in place by abject fear.

'I could stay up here all day,' John mused contentedly, pulling his pipe and a box of matches from his coat pocket.

'Doctor, if you please,' Mr. Tyson cautioned, 'no smoking in the balloon. The coal gas I use is less flammable than pure hydrogen, but that is no reason to take chances.'

'Oh, quite right,' John agreed, sheepishly returning the items to his pocket. 'Look there, Amelia,' he shouted, suddenly shifting his weight and tilting the entire basket in the process, 'you can make out the Palace!'

'John . . . please . . . don't . . . *do that*,' I managed to croak.

'Afraid of heights, Mrs. Watson?' Mr. Tyson asked.

'However can you tell?' I moaned sourly.

The aeronaut smiled, then leaned over the side of the basket (the sight of which alone nearly caused me to faint) and opened a box that was attached to the outside. After rummaging through it for a moment he pulled out a slender black telescope and extended it. 'Here, peer through this,' he said, handing it to me, 'it may help to reduce the feeling of height.'

So would landing, I thought, but I said nothing. With a quivering hand, I took the telescope.

'You will need both hands, I'm afraid.'

'But then I would have to let go of the ropes completely,' I said, in a terrified child's voice that I hardly recognised as my own.

'Don't worry, my dear, I shall steady you,' John said, carefully slipping an arm around my waist. Leaning against him, I actually began to feel more secure, enough so that I finally let go of the rope and put the telescope to my eye. Through the lens I was able to make details of Grosvenor Road and watched ant-like workmen crawling over the still-unfinished reconstruction of Vauxhall Bridge. Mr. Tyson's suggestion had proven quite astute: even though the bridge was far below us, its artificial proximity through the telescope did indeed restore some strength to my weakened legs.

'We appear to have company, Tyson,' John said, and taking my eye away from the telescope, I saw that another balloon, this one coloured a regal purple, was ascending rapidly to join us in mid-air, though it remained quite a distance off.

'That must be MacGregor,' Mr. Tyson said. 'He's new to the London Aero Club, though I believe he operated a balloon back in Scotland.'

It seemed to take little time for the purple balloon to rise to our level of height. Once it had, I levelled the spy glass in its direction. In its basket was a thin, bearded man — the pilot, obviously

33

— and a woman whose thin sporting outfit bordered on being too small to contain her fulsome figure. In addition, her wide white belt appeared to be cinched so tightly around her waist that I wondered how she could breathe. I could not see her features clearly, though she held her head high and with such practised determination that she seemed to be daring the wind to ruffle her dark hair.

As I watched, the man stepped behind her. He held something in his hands that I could not see clearly, but which he raised over the woman's head. Sunlight glinted off the object, which now looked like a taut wire. In a flash, his hands came down and around the woman's neck, and her head snapped backwards. The basket began to rock and jostle and the woman attempted, futilely, to fight off the attack. 'No!' I cried out, aware that I was standing here in total helplessness, watching as the man in the other balloon *strangled his passenger!*

Instinctively, I leapt out of John's protective hold and rashly bolted to the side of the basket, all the while keeping the telescope trained on the horrific act taking place in the other balloon.

'Amelia, what are you doing?' John cried, but I could not speak to answer. Now all I could see of the woman now was the back of her head as she slumped to the floor of the basket. The man was bearing down on her, his hands and arms like steel rods as he squeezed the life out of her!

'He's killing her!' I shouted. 'That man over there is killing a woman!'

'What? Where?' Mr. Tyson asked.

'In the purple balloon!' I cried, thrusting my hand out to point at it. But as I did, the telescope slipped from my grasp and disappeared into the void below. 'Oh,' I said, weakly.

'Well, at least it will fall into the river and not strike someone on the head,' Mr. Tyson sighed.

'Really, Amelia, this kind of hysteria is not like you at all,' John said.

'It is not every day that I witness a man killing a woman,' I replied.

John squinted in the sunlight in the

direction of the purple balloon. 'Well, I can see nothing of the sort.'

'Nor can I, without the telescope,' said Mr. Tyson. 'Let me see if I can raise him by voice.' From the bottom of the basket he picked up a huge megaphone, pointed it at the other balloon, and shouted, 'Ahoy! MacGregor, is that you?' After a few seconds, a faint voice came back: 'Yes. Is that you, Tyson?'

'It is. Who is aloft with you?'

There was a pause of several seconds before the answer came: 'My wife.'

'Is she all right?'

Another pause, during which I heard only the beating of my own heart. Then a much lighter and higher voice came across the winds. 'Yes, I am fine. Why do you ask?'

My mouth opened to say something, but no words came out.

'We thought we saw a sign of distress,' Mr. Tyson shouted, 'but obviously we were in error. A pleasant day to you.' With that, he set down the megaphone and regarded me with a look of amused condescension.

'Please do not try to tell me that I was mistaken,' I said. 'I distinctly saw the man strangling the woman.'

'Well, if I ever decide to strangle my wife, I hope she will take it with similar equanimity,' Mr. Tyson said. The crack drew a hearty chuckle from John, though I found it singularly unamusing.

'Mr. Tyson,' I said, evenly, 'I would consider it a personal favour if you would return this contraption to earth so that I can report what I saw to the police. Perhaps they will listen to me instead of making jokes at my expense.'

'Oh, really, Amelia,' John said, 'we heard the woman's voice!'

'We heard *someone's* voice,' I corrected. 'It could have been the man imitating a woman's voice.'

John sighed. 'Perhaps we should indeed go down, Tyson. I can see that my wife has become too upset to enjoy the rest of the journey.'

As though I had been enjoying it thus far! I thought, but remained silent.

'As you wish,' the balloonist replied. 'The wind is against us for a return to

Ranelagh Gardens, though I should be able to set her down in Vauxhall, across the river. Even the most skilled balloonist is at the mercy of the winds, I'm afraid.'

Despite his admonishment, Mr. Tyson proved to be an exceptionally skilled balloonist, tugging periodically on the descent rope until we were hanging ten or twelve metres above the river. For a few fraught moments I was afraid we were going to splash down in the middle of the Thames, but Mr. Tyson's careful attention to the direction of the wind, combined with his knowledge of descent, landed us with a *thump* on the Grand Walk of Vauxhall Gardens. A large crowd of spectators circled us as he tugged another rope, which instantly deflated the balloon. As John helped me out of the basket, I heard a man from the crowd yell: 'Look, here comes another one!' Following the gaze of the spectators upward, I saw another balloon descending for a landing nearby. It was the purple balloon!

'The murderous brute is going to land next to us!' I cried.

'Good,' John declared, 'that way we can settle this issue of so-called murder once and for all. We shall go over and see it down, and if there is no woman to be seen, I will accompany you to the Yard and stay with you while you make your report. If, however, both the man and the woman are there, I want you to admit that you saw something which you only misinterpreted as an attack. Agreed?'

'Well . . . let's go and see it down, darling,' I said. The basket of the purple balloon was now skittering over the tops of the trees and heading for a spot in the midst of the growing crowd, which parted to allow for landing room. It came down with a much more violent bump than had ours, and the crowd seemed to delight in the balloon's sudden deflation into a lifeless, purple caul. I, on the other hand, was more concerned with the two — yes, *two* — people in the basket.

'You see?' John said. 'They are both there.'

'Oh, I see very clearly, darling,' I replied, 'and that woman is not the same one I saw through the telescope.'

'*Not the same* — !' John blurted out, before catching himself in the gaze of more than a few startled onlookers. 'Amelia, I am beginning to worry about you.'

'I know what I saw, John! This woman is slender whereas the other one was plump. And this one's hair is different, too — lighter, more auburn.'

'Both her hair colour and build could have been distorted by the distance and the telescope lens,' he replied.

I had to admit that it sounded logical, though it was hard to imagine how the woman's newfound slenderness could be solely the result of lens distortion. The tight black belt that encircled her waist under her full bosom made her look almost waspish, not at all like the figure I had seen aloft. Despite all logic, there was still something wrong, but I could not put my finger on what it was.

That elusive detail continued to torment me even as we prepared for bed that evening.

'You are still fretting about that incident in the balloon, aren't you?' John sighed as he donned his night clothes.

'I know what I saw, dear,' I said, wearily.

'You know, Amelia, altitude has been known to affect some people, even to the point of altering their perception.' He gently placed his hands on my shoulders. 'Had I known you were susceptible to such an effect, I would not have badgered you to join me. I am sorry, my dear.'

I leaned against him and felt his arms slide around me, enjoying the comfort of his strength. 'And I am sorry too, darling, for ruining your birthday treat.'

'Oh, it was hardly ruined. I had a glorious time.'

'I'm glad. Still, I wish I could bring to the surface whatever it is that bothered me about seeing that woman on the ground,' I persisted. 'Until I can do that, I shall probably not be able to sleep.'

'And I wish I could make you accept the black-and-white facts. MacGregor and his wife went up in the balloon and they came down again a few hours later.'

'Very well, John, I don't wish to talk

about it any . . . oh!' My hand uncon-sciously went to my forehead.

'Amelia, what is it?'

'The thing that has been bothering me, a fact in *black-and-white*, as you yourself said. The woman I saw in the balloon wore a white belt. But the woman who landed in the balloon, even though she was similarly dressed in a sporting outfit, wore a *black* belt. Why on earth would someone change her belt while flying in a balloon?'

'Perhaps the white one broke,' John reasoned.

'So she carries a spare belt around in case the one she's wearing breaks? I'm sorry, darling, it won't do. There had to be two women in that balloon.'

'But really, Amelia, you are asking me to believe that somehow this MacGregor killed his wife, disposed of the body, and then produced another woman to take her place, all in mid-air!'

'I never said it was not an ingenious plot.'

'*Impossible* is more like it,' he har-rumphed. 'Try to get some rest, dear. We can continue this discussion tomorrow when our heads are clear.'

Despite my earlier fears, I had no trouble sleeping that night. The next morning, over breakfast, John and I chatted amiably on a variety of topics, and I never once mentioned the 'impossible' murder. Just before he left for his surgery, though, John turned to me and cautioned: 'Amelia, I hope that you are not thinking of rushing to the police as soon as I am out of the door with your tale of a witnessed murder.'

'How could I?' I asked, innocently. 'I have no real evidence.'

'Please refrain from trying to produce any,' he admonished, and I acknowledged his concern with my most guileless expression. But the moment he had left I was on the telephone — not to the police, as John feared, but instead to the London Aero Club. Within a minute, I was connected with the club's secretary, and shortly after that, to Mr. Tyson himself.

'Mr. Tyson, this is Amelia Watson,' I announced. 'You took my husband and me up yesterday.'

'Oh, yes, you were the one who witnessed the strangling.' I could hear him chuckling. 'I relayed your story to MacGregor, who took it with amusement.'

'You *told* him?' I cried.

'Yes, and he explained that his wife had lost her balance at one point and had indeed fallen down in the basket. You must have seen that and misinterpreted it.'

'What would you say, Mr. Tyson, if I told you that I am more convinced than ever that there were two women, and that the woman who landed in the balloon was not the woman I saw being attacked?' I went on to tell him about the conflicting belts.

'Belts, you say?' Mr. Tyson replied. 'Mrs. Watson, can you come down here to the club this afternoon? There is something I would like to show you, which you may find interesting.'

Since he would not elaborate over the telephone what he wished me to see, some three hours later I arrived by hansom at Ranelagh Gardens, and made

44

my way to a converted stable in which the members of the Aero Club stored their balloons.

Mr. Tyson greeted me at the door and led me inside, where a half-dozen men were tending to their balloons, which were deflated and heaped in great, colourful piles and set inside individual stalls. Coiled up in one corner was the large hose used to pump the coal gas out of the city main into the huge inflatables. 'Come this way,' he said.

'What is it you wish to show me?' I asked.

'Proof that your imagination is more vivid than your memory,' he responded, which was *not* what I wanted to hear. I was on the verge of protesting when we arrived at the stall containing his balloon. Setting the basket upright, he said, 'Let me start with a question: how tall was the woman you saw through the telescope?'

'I can only tell you relatively,' I replied. 'I recall her being shorter than the man by several inches.'

'Remember that,' he said, climbing inside the basket and removing his jacket.

'Step back a few yards,' he instructed, and I did so. 'Now, Mrs. Watson, what colour is the belt I am wearing?'

'I am afraid I cannot see it. It is covered by the top edge of the — oh, dear.'

Smiling, Mr. Tyson nimbly vaulted out of the basket. 'You see my point, Mrs. Watson? I am five feet ten inches tall, roughly the same height as MacGregor, and even for someone of my height, the top of the basket still obscures my waist. For a woman who was several inches shorter, seeing her belt would be virtually impossible.'

'Then how do you explain my seeing it?' I asked.

'I don't, Mrs. Watson,' Mr. Tyson replied. 'I am merely pointing out the facts.'

Yes, and it was yet another 'fact' that contradicted what I *knew* I saw! I began to massage my aching head and said, quietly: 'Thank you, Mr. Tyson, for your time. I shall take my leave now.'

I started for the door but stopped when I saw a man coming my way, a figure I recognised immediately — it was

MacGregor, the murderer! He gave a gentlemanly tip of his hat as he passed me and then marched straight to another balloon stall in which his basket was located. I heard Mr. Tyson call out: 'Hey, Mac, will you be taking your wife up again this Sunday?'

I dallied in the doorway, hoping to hear the answer.

'No, she's gone, left this morning to visit her family up north,' Mr. MacGregor answered, his voice betraying his Scottish roots. 'Dinnae know when she'll be back.'

I slipped out of the building and crossed the park green, my mind racing. The villain's diabolical plan had become all too clear: to get rid of his wife, he takes her up in a balloon, which is a very public event, then kills her in the air, gets rid of the body and has another woman take her place for the landing. Now, a day later, he explains his wife's absence by spreading the story that she has gone indefinitely to visit family, a story that no one would question since there were so many witnesses who could claim to have seen the woman the day before she disappeared. And how cleverly the brute chose to land in a different park, so that no one who saw the launch would be present for the landing, therefore leaving no one who could identify 'Mrs. MacGregor' as two different women.

No one except me.

But how had he done it? How had the man switched women two thousand feet above ground?

I knew I was going to have to discuss my encounter at the Aero Club with John that evening, although I was not looking forward to it. On the other hand, I had only promised him that I would not go to the police; I had said nothing about speaking to Mr. Tyson.

As it turned out, that made little difference to John's reaction. 'Amelia, Amelia, Amelia,' he moaned, resting his head in his hands, 'you actually went to Tyson with this ridiculous theory of yours? Must you alienate *all* my friends?'

'John, that is unfair,' I said, stung more deeply than I cared to admit. I knew he had been harbouring resentment since I had all but demanded that Mr. Holmes leave our home after a torturous two-month stay. As a result, the detective had packed up and left, childishly refusing to tell John where he was going, if he even knew.

'You are right, it was unfair. I am sorry, my dear,' John said. 'But please refrain from hatching penny dreadful plots and take a look at the facts. The only proof you can offer for your theory is this business of differing belts, yet by your own account, Tyson has proven to you that seeing the belt in the air was impossible.'

'It was not impossible, John, because I saw it.'

'Fine, perhaps she was standing on a table in a balloon basket and that is why you saw her belt,' he cried in exasperation. 'There is still the problem of where he hid the second woman. Even if she was lying curled up on the bottom of the basket, she would have been seen by the . . . the . . . oh, Great Scott . . . ' His voice trailed off.

He needed to say no more, for in the same instant, I too realised how it had been done. 'It fits, John, it all fits!' I exclaimed, marvelling at how such a baffling, 'impossible' crime was accomplished through such an utterly simple trick.

'We must contact the Yard immediately,' John cried, adding: 'By the way, I will never doubt you again.' He was already up and out of his chair and had the telephone in his hand when I stopped him.

'Not yet,' I told him. 'We need to make absolutely certain we are right first. I suggest we visit the storage facility of the Aero Club ourselves before bringing in the police.'

Within minutes the two of us were being driven through the city southward to Ranelagh Gardens. By the time we had reached the Chelsea Bridge Road the sky had turned to black velvet and a night chill had descended upon the city. We stepped out of the hansom at the entrance to the park, and I quickly led John to the converted stable, the door of which was unlocked.

'Do you think anyone is inside?' I whispered.

'From the looks of the place, I doubt it,' John whispered back. We stepped inside, which was completely dark, and since neither of us had thought to bring a torch, John lit a match. Once my eyes adjusted to the dim light, I pointed out the stall containing MacGregor's balloon, and we crept toward it. The match burnt down and John lit another one. We had no sooner reached the stall when the inside of the stable became awash with glaring electric light.

'Stop where you are,' a voice called out, and squinting through the sudden brightness, I could make out the form of a man, who was holding a club of some kind. As he stepped nearer, I could see it was Mr. Tyson!

'Oh, it is you, Doctor,' he replied, lowering the club. 'For heaven's sake, man, extinguish that match!'

John quickly puffed it out, and muttered: 'We thought the place was deserted.'

'So it would have been,' the balloonist said. 'I was just about to leave when I noticed two figures sneaking around outside. I thought you were MacGregor and the woman posing as his wife.'

'You mean, the second woman?' I asked, a note of triumph in my voice.

'Exactly,' Mr. Tyson replied. 'I couldn't quite expel from my mind what you said this afternoon, Mrs. Watson. Your utter conviction that you had seen a murder, combined with the convenient absence of Mrs. MacGregor, started me thinking; but only after I'd left the club did it strike me that, taken completely at face value, everything you described made sense. So I came back to see for myself. Why are you to here?'

'For the same reason,' John stated, explaining our theory.

Mr. Tyson nodded. 'Come take a look, then.' Reaching into MacGregor's basket, he thrust a finger into a tiny hole in the floor — or at least what appeared to be the floor. With a quick tug, the balloonist pulled up the false floor to reveal a concealed compartment underneath.

'So this is where the second woman hid,' John muttered.

'It couldn't have been comfortable,'

Mr. Tyson said, 'but I imagine that did not matter much. MacGregor and his wife stood on the false floor for their journey, which is why her belt was visible. She was about a foot higher than normal.'

'And once he thought he was out of sight of anything except birds,' I went on, 'he killed her and then opened the compartment to allow the second woman out. The two of them then placed the body under the false floor and kept it there, presumably until it was safe to remove it.'

'You presume correctly, you damned, nosy snoop!' said a voice from behind us. The three of us spun around to see MacGregor, armed with a pistol, standing beside the second woman, the one I had seen land in Vauxhall Park.

'Andrew, be careful,' the woman said, clearly frightened.

'Put the gun down, MacGregor,' commanded Mr. Tyson.

'And have you alive to ruin my plans?' the villain responded. 'I mean to escape, Jack, make a new life for myself with Mary here. It'll be a happy life, not like the one I'm leaving behind. I'm out now, out of a terrible marriage and a failing business that were forced on me, and for the first time in my life, free! I will nae let anything or anyone stand in my way!'

'You can't shoot us all in cold blood!' I cried, indignantly.

MacGregor's face took on an expression of frantic determination. 'I dinnae have a choice,' he said, levelling the pistol at my chest.

'No, Andrew!' Mary declared, grabbing his arm and forcing it upwards so that his first shot lodged in the ceiling.

'Damn you, Mary!' MacGregor shouted. 'Let go!'

'No!' she screamed back. 'I went along with Hetty's murder because it meant we could finally be together, but this is different!'

'Let go!' he demanded, slapping the woman and knocking her to the ground.

'Andrew . . . ' she sobbed.

'Oh, God, forgive me, Mary,' he pleaded, turning his attention away from us long enough for John to charge him and attempt to wrest the gun from his hand. But MacGregor proved to be too strong. He threw John off himself as though he weighed no more than a child, sending my husband sprawling on the floor. Then MacGregor pointed the gun at his face, and I screamed. In the chaos that followed, all I recall is Mary leaping up from the ground and rushing to MacGregor, screaming 'Nooo!', a shot firing, and then the sight of her slumping to the ground, a red stain appearing on the front of her blue linen dress.

'Mary!' MacGregor wailed, as Mr. Tyson tackled him from behind. In the struggle, another wild shot was fired. An instant later, there was a blast inside the building that knocked all of us to the floor.

'Good God, man, you've hit the gas hose!' Tyson cried. 'Get out of here!' While I wanted nothing more than to comply, I was too stricken with both shock and panic to move. A second later I felt myself literally being picked up and carried through the door and into the night by John's strong arms.

Mr. Tyson dashed out behind us. 'The

whole building could go up,' he panted. 'Where's MacGregor?'

'Still inside,' John said, setting me down.

Rushing back to the door, Mr. Tyson shouted: 'MacGregor, get out of there! You'll be killed!'

'I'm a dead man already, Jack,' an anguished voice called from inside the building.

Mr. Tyson tried calling to his friend again, but another explosion ripped through the building and a plume of orange flame burst through the roof. 'Get away from here!' Mr. Tyson commanded, and the three of us ran as fast as we could toward the park's entrance. When the final blast came, it sounded like the end of the world.

'Good Lord,' was all John could manage, staring in the distance at the eerie, flickering glow.

We stayed until the first of the fire brigade lorries arrived, then we drifted away.

I was still suffering from shock somewhat when John and I returned home. After a very stiff whisky, which John encouraged me to down, I began to recover. It was only later, as we lay in bed that the shock fully subsided and gave way to a sudden rush of tears. John tried to comfort me, but he did not understand the source of my distress. 'None of this would have happened if I had not seen what I was never meant to see,' I moaned.

'Who knows, Amelia,' John said gently, 'perhaps you were meant to see it.'

'What do you mean?'

'We choose to believe that each of us are in control of our own lives, but perhaps we are not. Perhaps we are no more responsible for what happens to us than ... I don't know ... than the characters in a book. Perhaps it was your destiny to stop MacGregor.'

'Perhaps it was,' I murmured, closing my eyes and wishing for the veil of sleep.

The Adventure of The Bleak House Fire

Even if one did not know that the man in the bowler hat who was approaching our table at the restaurant was a CID inspector from Scotland Yard, the natural authority that he exuded might have given the fact away.

'Great Scott, Laurie, what brings you here?' asked my husband.

'I went to your home and your maid told me you were dining here this evening,' said Inspector Laurie. 'Dr. Watson, I have need of your assistance.'

'At this moment?'

'As soon as you can comply, sir.'

'Very well,' John said, setting down his fork.

While I hated to abandon my rather excellent sole fillet, I said, 'Let me signal for the waiter to bring the bill and then we shall be at your disposal, Inspector.'

He coughed a touch too loudly before saying, 'Actually, Mrs. Watson, I am in need of the doctor alone. I require his medical expertise, and the circumstances of this particular case are so, well, *gruesome* is the only word, that I cannot in good conscience expose a woman to them.'

'Gracious,' I muttered. 'I suppose I will find my way back home, then.'

'Thank you, Mrs. Watson,' the inspector said. 'Whenever you are ready, Doctor.'

I finished my dinner alone and, as I had promised, returned home to engage myself in what was becoming my true occupation: awaiting my husband's return. It came shortly before eleven. Oddly, John's handsome face was marked not so much by grimness as perturbation. 'Please do not keep me in suspense any longer, darling,' I said, rushing to him. 'What is the great and terrible mystery?'

'Tommyrot, is what it is,' John said. 'I cannot believe that a man as experienced as Laurie would entertain such an idea even for a second! It is pure codswallop, and I told the man so!' He forcefully took off his coat and hat and tossed them onto the coat rack.

'Good heavens, darling, I have rarely seen you in such a state,' I commented.

'Perhaps it is my own fault,' he went on. 'Perhaps I have so convinced people that I am nothing but a sounding board for Holmes' brilliance that they now think I am dim enough to believe anything.'

'John, please, tell me what it was that upset you so?' I begged.

He cast his gaze on me, and his face softened. 'Very well,' he said, pouring himself a whiskey and carrying it to the sofa. 'Laurie was not exaggerating the gruesomeness of the scene,' he began. 'It was the upper room of a dilapidated boarding house. There was a dead man in it . . . or so we think.'

'You are not certain that he was dead?'

'We are not certain that he was a man. The preliminary identification was based upon the fact that there was evidence of an old fracture on the ankle of the foot, which coincided with the testimony of the landlord that the man had once spoken of having sustained a broken ankle in his younger days. I examined the left foot and did indeed find evidence of a healed fracture. Still, I would hate to have to testify in court that the identification is conclusive.'

'Was there no way to identify the rest of him?'

John stared at his glass, then spoke: 'Amelia, there was no rest of him.'

'Oh, dear,' I said. 'The man's foot had been severed?'

'No, it had been burnt off. Elsewhere on the bed was a pile of ashes, roughly in the shape of a supine figure.'

'Was the bed not destroyed?'

'Nothing in the room was destroyed, only the body.'

'But how could that be?' I asked. 'Oh dear, I know how . . . spontaneous combustion!'

John looked at me as though I had suddenly turned into a giraffe. 'Not you too, Amelia!' he cried. '*Please* do not tell me that you believe in such balderdash! It is bad enough hearing it from Laurie!'

'Darling, I've not really given it that much thought. I am only aware of the phenomenon through reading Charles Dickens. It is mentioned, I believe, in *Bleak House.*'

'And that is precisely where it belongs, in fiction. It has absolutely no merit or factuality in the real world.'

'How do you explain the fire, then?'

John downed his whiskey. 'Clearly someone carefully staged the scene in order to create a conundrum, somehow procuring the foot of the poor unfortunate, and carrying it up to the room along with a supply of ashes, which were arranged in the form of a body. I attempted to explain that to Laurie, but he kept speaking about a human being suddenly bursting into flames for no reason. It is absurd!' Setting his glass down, he rose and started toward the bedroom. 'I am turning in, Amelia. I am exhausted.'

'I shall be in shortly, dear,' I said.

Did I believe in spontaneous combustion? John was the authority on all things medical, not I, so if he said it was impossible, I had to give credence to his opinion. On the other hand, I knew Inspector Laurie well enough to realise that he was not given to flights of fancy. And then there was Mr. Dickens, in whose judgment I tend to trust implicitly. Perhaps, I thought, as I switched off the sitting room lamp, it would do well if I were to speak with Inspector Laurie and hear his side of the argument.

The next morning, after John had gone off on his appointed rounds (and whether he was consulting with a medical patient, seeing his publisher, or connecting with the booking agent regarding his new-found career on the lecture stage, I had no idea), I set out to the Thames-side edifice of New Scotland Yard, arriving there just in time to pull Inspector Laurie away from his workload and shuttle him into a nearby coffee house. It was the least I could do to repay him for disrupting our dinner the evening before.

'I hear you and John had a disagreement last evening,' I began.

The inspector allowed himself a slight smile. 'That is putting it mildly, Mrs.

Watson,' he said. 'We responded to a call from the landlord and found what appeared to be a body burnt to ash, yet the rest of the room was intact. It was one of my sergeants who mentioned spontaneous combustion. Apparently there is a case or two of it on record. But your husband reacted to that theory as violently as if I were advocating that England become an American state.'

'He is not very tolerant of spiritualism either,' I said.

'His theory was that the body, what there was of it, was planted there to make it look like spontaneous combustion. That is, of course, completely possible, though it strikes me as an overly elaborate ruse. Mrs. Watson, might I prevail upon you to accompany me to the scene of the man's death?'

I must admit, that took me by surprise. 'I had somehow convinced myself that you were trying to keep me away.'

'Only while the body, what little there was of it, was present. It has since been removed.'

'Still, you are asking for my assistance?

Inspector Laurie, I am quite flattered.'

He sighed in a resigned sort of way. 'Mrs. Watson, if you ask me to track a thief, I could do it. If you ask me to solve a murder that has been done with a pistol or knife, I'm your man. But every now and then a case comes along that demands more imagination than the average copper, even the average Scotland Yard inspector, can muster. With Holmes no longer available for consultation and your husband momentarily refusing to lend his assistance, there is no one else to whom I can turn.'

Now I was positively blushing.

The inspector was as good as his word and within an hour we were inside the dark, cramped attic room that had been inhabited by the dead man, whom had been identified as one Bob Usher. Indeed, the scene of the man's death was exactly as Inspector Laurie had described: a threadbare bedspread was scorched, but not consumed, and even though the mortal remains had been removed, I could still make out the shape of a man. Near the bottom of the grotesque shadow, I spotted a yellowish stain.

'That is tallow,' Inspector Laurie said, 'most likely from over there.' He pointed to a tarnished brass candelabrum with places for three candles, though there were only two in it, sitting atop a battered dresser, next to a simple crucifix. 'Since there was no electricity in this room, either candle or lamp was the only light source. And I know what you are thinking, Mrs. Watson, but if that candle had started the blaze, the bedspread would have burnt as well.'

'Couldn't someone have come in while the man was sleeping and set him ablaze?'

Inspector Laurie shook his head. 'This door is the only entryway into and out of the room, and it was bolted from the inside. Two of my men had to break it down for us to gain entry. No assailant could have done as you have suggested and got away leaving the door bolted.'

'Could he have doused himself with something?' I asked.

'If he had, there would have been evidence of it, such as a can with the residue of the fluid. There is nothing.'

I had to admit, it was the kind of puzzle that Mr. Holmes would be sorry to have missed. The question was, what, if anything, could I actually do in the way of illuminating the dark mystery? At that moment, though, my thoughts were suddenly turned away from the mystery and to the sound of footsteps coming up the stairs outside the room. Inspector Laurie heard them, too. He motioned to me to step back out of the sight range of the door, and the two of us waited silently to see who was approaching. Before we saw anyone, we heard a woman's voice call: 'Hullo? Is someone in there?'

Inspector Laurie stepped out. 'Scotland Yard, madam,' he said. 'Might I ask who you are?'

The woman who stepped into the room was slender, with jet-black hair that was pulled severely into a bun at the back of her head. She did not appear to be very old, but had a careworn face which looked incapable of breaking into merriment. 'I am Gemma Usher,' she announced. 'This is my uncle's room.'

The inspector's eyebrows rose. 'Indeed? Do you know what occurred here?'

'I know that my uncle is dead,' she said. 'Burnt, I am told.'

'Forgive me for saying so,' Inspector Laurie went on, 'but you do not seem unduly upset by his death.'

'I did not know him well. In fact, I had not seen nor heard from him in close to fifteen years, prior to his writing to me with this address. He sent a letter saying that he wanted to see me, and that he had something for me, though I have no idea what it might be. I first came to this house three days ago and knocked upon his door, but it was locked. I came back three times, but each time it was the same: the door bolted and the room silent behind it. He must have already been dead. Then yesterday I came back and learned what had happened.'

'Do you have any idea why he wished to see you?'

'None, I'm afraid. Honestly, Officer —'

'Inspector, madam.'

'Of course, Inspector — I have no idea whatever. Up until receiving his note, I had no confirmation that he was still alive.'

'And why,' I chimed in, 'did you come here today?'

The woman looked at me. 'I'm sorry?'

'You say that you learned yesterday that your uncle was dead, so you cannot have come here with the thought of seeing him. Why, then, did you come?'

'Are you with Scotland Yard as well?' Gemma Usher asked me.

'No, she is not,' Inspector Laurie said, 'though if you require official credentials before you answer the question, allow me to repeat it. Why did you come here today?'

'Inspector, as my uncle's only remaining relative, the disposition of his goods is now entrusted to me. Mr. Cruffins, the landlord of this building, made it quite clear that he wishes this room to be emptied and made available for re-letting as soon as is possible. I came to see if I might start moving his things out.'

'Of course,' the inspector said. 'Though I daresay it will not take long to clear out.'

'No, my uncle was not a man of

means,' the woman acknowledged. 'I imagine I need your permission to proceed, however.'

'I don't envision a problem on our end, though I would like at least another day.'

'Very well,' the woman sighed. 'Please contact me as soon as you are finished. I am at number twelve, Cartwell Gardens. Good day, Inspector.' With a curt nod to me, she took her leave.

'Bit of a chilly one, that,' the inspector said when she was gone, and I was inclined to agree. 'There's not much more to be seen here,' he sighed. 'I suppose there's nothing left to do but record Usher's death as an act of God and have done with it. I'm sorry to have wasted your time, Mrs. Watson.'

We left the premises and Inspector Laurie kindly offered me a cab back home. But once back in Queen Anne Street, my mind remained focused on the conundrum of the non-burnt room, and when John returned home several hours later, I was ready for him.

'Darling,' I began, 'I went to see Inspector Laurie today.'

'Did you?' he huffed. 'I imagine he is trying to use you to persuade me to accept that preposterous theory of his.'

'Not at all,' I went on. 'In fact, he readily admits that his theory is flawed, and even now would welcome your assistance. My feeling is that he is simply following Mr. Holmes' dictum about eliminating the impossible so that the improbable remains the only explanation.'

'Spontaneous combustion *is* impossible!' John declared. 'If he is emulating Holmes, then he must eliminate that straight off.'

'But what does that leave?'

John snorted. 'Oh, for heaven's sake, Amelia, you are not going to let this drop, are you?'

'You must admit, darling, it is puzzling.'

'Very well,' John sighed. 'Let us look at the facts: the man was living in a run-down rooming house in a rather disreputable area of the city. What does that suggest to you?'

'That he was poor?'

'Naturally, but what is a common trait

of a man who down on his heels?'

I shook my head.

'Drink, Amelia. It is one of the biggest reasons for a man's inability to hold a situation. Now, then, let us presume that the fellow was indeed a drunkard — '

'But there were no bottles inside the room,' I interrupted.

John smiled. 'Ah, but did you happen to notice the gin shop that was located a door or two down from the building?'

I had to admit that I had not.

'The man goes to the gin shop with whatever funds he has, drinks himself senseless, goes back to his room, perhaps lights a candle, falls unconscious, the lit candle falls upon him and sets his clothing ablaze, and because the man's system is so permeated with combustible alcohol, the fire continues to burn until the man is totally consumed, or nearly so.'

'John, have you told this to the inspector?'

'Well, no. Until you prompted the thought just now, I had not even considered it.'

'Darling, we must tell him . . . although . . . '

'Although what?'

'Wouldn't even a man so inebriated that he falls unconscious be summoned back to clarity through immolation?'

'One would think so,' John agreed, 'though perhaps he did not simply fall unconscious on the bed. Perhaps his system gave out altogether. He died, and then the fire began. The body, thoroughly permeated with alcohol, would burn very slowly — smoulder, in fact — until it was completely consumed!'

'That is brilliant, John!' I cried. 'A bit sickening, but brilliant. We must tell the inspector.'

'No, not yet,' he said, surprising me. 'Not until we have proof.'

'Proof?'

'Yes. I would like to do more investigation on this case in order to provide Laurie with as complete a solution as possible. That way, he will be unable to deny it.' Before I fully understood what was happening, my now-ebullient husband had virtually pulled me out of home and onto the street, where we were embarking on a journey to The Crawling Man, the name of the disreputable-looking tavern near the late Mr. Usher's boarding house.

While I am not personally averse to entering public houses, The Crawling Man was another matter entirely. It was the kind of establishment that I was not aware still existed: dark, dingy, dirty and so reeking of stale tobacco that I had to hold a kerchief over my face. There were only two customers inside, a man and an elderly woman, and both might have been mistaken for cadavers had they not been coughing.

'Perhaps I should wait for you outside, John,' I said, distastefully.

'There is nothing to fear, my dear,' he replied, then he rapped on the shabby counter and called, 'Landlord!'

A thin, sallow man limped out from behind a curtain and looked at us dubiously. 'Don't get many coves in 'ere,' he drawled.

'Understandably so,' John said, 'but I am not here for a drink, I am here for information. What do you know about Bob Usher?'

The man spat on the floor and answered: 'Glad 'e's dead.'

John's eyebrows disappeared under the brim of his hat. 'Indeed?' he uttered.

'Aye. Chased away some o' my best customers. Come in here preachin' the evils of hard drink, and not jus' once, but time after time. 'E'd go so far as t'offer t'pay folks t'lay off the stuff. Near put me out o' business.'

'What a tragedy that would have been,' I muttered through my kerchief.

'Aye,' the landlord agreed, oblivious to irony. Meanwhile, I noticed that John's face had fallen, and not from the atmosphere of the place. 'So, you mean to say that Mr. Usher himself did not drink?'

'Not a drop,' the sallow man affirmed, capping it with a muttered oath. 'Sober as a bleedin' judge.'

'I see,' John muttered. 'Thank you. Come along, Amelia.' I was more than grateful to take my leave of the horrendous tavern, and we nearly made it outside when another voice piped up: 'Hey, guv, I'll tell you about Bob Usher, if you like.'

We looked over and saw the slow, painful rise of a wizened man who had been lying out of sight on a bench near the entrance. 'For a price, of course.'

John returned to the bar to purchase a glass of gin, which he handed to the man, who downed it in one gulp. He opened his toothless mouth to talk, but before he could begin I begged that we step outside. Once out of the suffocating vapours of the gin shop, I vowed never to complain about the London air again.

The name of our newfound friend, we learned, was Sandy Wicking. 'Bob was a right fine fellow, if you ask me,' he said. 'Always good for a touch if you needed doss, always willing to help those less fortunate than himself.'

'You make it sound as though he were a man of means,' I said.

'Right-o.'

'But how can that be?' John demanded. 'The man lived like a pauper, and I refuse to believe that he was not a drinker!'

'Well, he was, once,' Mr. Wicking said. 'Then he came in to his money and changed. See, old Bob bumps into a vicar on the street one night, and this vicar takes sum of his condition and tells him that if he were to stop drinking and put what little money he had to better use, the Almighty would reward him. Well, Bob figures he's got nothing to lose, so he skips the bar that night and goes instead to buy himself a ticket for the Irish Sweepstakes. And blimey if he didn't win.'

'How much did he get?' I asked.

The man stopped to wipe his mouth with the back of his hand, then said: 'I don't rightly know, but I heard it was in the thousands.'

'Good Lord,' John uttered. 'Why, then, did he stay in that hovel?'

'Well, Bob is convinced that vicar was right, and that he was rewarded by the Almighty. So he sets about trying to persuade others to follow his example and collect their reward. He never spent a farthing of those winnings on himself, near as I could see. Wore the same clothing, still dined on oysters, and probably still used a candle for a crow. Only difference was that he lost his taste for gin, even strong beer, and from that day on never touched a drop of the stuff.'

'Never?'

'Never, guv.'

'When was the last time you saw him?' I asked.

'I don't know . . . maybe a week past, no more than that. He came in the place here and started to preach, and Ginny Pete ran him off, told him he never wanted to see him again.'

Ginny Pete, I presumed, was the emaciated landlord.

Mr. Wicking went on: 'Then later that night he . . . wait a minute . . . now I remember it . . . I saw him with another bloke after the shop here closed. They were going up to Bob's room, and Bob, he was walking kind of wobbly, like he was sick, or maybe hurt. As a matter of fact, I heard him blurt out something about his legs, or his knees, like they were hurting him. It was his knees, now that I think of it. Hurt by his own knees, he said.'

I had a sudden grim vision of a

smouldering fire beginning to spontane-
ously generate within the poor man's legs,
but I daren't voice it to John, who was
now asking: 'Could you see who the other
man was?'

The little man screwed up his face in
thought, then shook his head. 'No, didn't
see the face. Just a bloke in a long coat
and a slouch hat.'

'Was the man heavy or thin?' John
asked, and I knew where his question was
leading.

'Thin, I'd say,' Sandy replied.

'Can you remember anything else
about him?' I asked. 'The colour of his
hair, for instance?'

'No, it was too dark, and with the hat,
and all . . . ' He ran his hand over his
mouth. 'You know, guv, all this talking has
made my throat a bit dry, and . . . '

John pulled a sixpence from his pocket
and tossed it toward the little man, who
deftly caught it, gave a parody of a salute,
and then dashed back into the gin shop.
'Well,' my husband said, 'it would appear
this case is solved.'

'It is?' I responded.

'Certainly, Amelia. Didn't you hear what the man said? That Usher was walking wobbly, like he was sick, or perhaps hurt. But he was not sick or hurt, Amelia. He was sodden, so incapacitated by drink that he could barely walk.'

'But I thought the man was a teetotaller.'

'He became one, my dear, but prior to that, he drank as much as anyone else in his position. It is not unreasonable to believe that he had fallen back to his old ways — with help, of course.'

'Help?' I asked.

'Don't you see, Amelia? Ginny Pete was the man in the hat and coat who was seen escorting Usher back to his room. Incensed over the business he had lost through Usher's impromptu lectures, he decided to get rid of him. I imagine he got the man drunk and then set him ablaze.'

'All well and good, dear, but how did he manage to do it and still bolt the door from the inside?'

'Well . . . er, I don't know, though once the inspector has interrogated the man, I am sure the story will come out.'

'Perhaps,' I said.

'You sound doubtful, Amelia,' John said, rather stiffly.

'No, darling, not doubtful, it's just that . . . John, do you know what that little man meant when he said Usher still used . . . what was it . . . a candle for a crow?'

'Oh, probably some form of rhyming slang, I would imagine. Now, then, shall we go to the Yard?'

'I suppose we must . . . *oh!*' I reached for my forehead.

'What is it Amelia?' John asked, then he narrowed his eyes. 'Ordinarily, that gesture would indicate that you have suddenly been struck by a realisation regarding the case, but there is nothing left to deduce here.'

'But, John . . . oh, I had a sudden sharp pain in my head, is all,' I lied, because I had, indeed, made a connection based on something that I had heard. 'It was probably a delayed reaction to all the smoke in that gin shop. You know my aversion to tobacco. Darling, you go to see Inspector Laurie, while I go home.'

'Very well. I shall hail a cab for you.'

He strode down the street and flagged down the first available hansom, which I stepped into. But once the driver had pulled away from the curb, I gave a different address than ours in Queen Anne Street. I had to be certain of my suspicion.

The streets were heavily congested, not only with people and horse carts, but also an alarming number of those dreadful, spluttering motorcars. Heaven help the Empire if they take over the byways completely! It took some forty-five minutes to arrive at our destination. I paid the driver and knocked on the door of Number 12, Cartwell Gardens. A voice behind the door called: 'Who is it?'

'My name is Amelia Watson,' I called back. 'We met yesterday in the rooms of your uncle. I was with Inspector Laurie.'

'What do you want?' the voice came again.

'I want you to open this door.'

After a pause, I heard the lock slide, and the door creaked open. The thin woman peeked out. 'I am busy,' she said.

'Miss Usher,' I began, 'I have come to appeal to your good nature to turn yourself in, before an innocent man is arrested.'

'What on earth are you raving on about?'

'Please, Miss Usher, I am not much in the mood for sparring. I know you facilitated the death of your uncle. I don't know exactly how, but I am convinced that you did it, and I believe I know why: his newfound fortune. You may talk to me about it or talk to the police. It is your choice.'

'You are mad!' she cried. 'I never asked my uncle for anything, certainly not his money!'

'Then you admit that you know of his sweepstakes winnings?' I asked, and her mouth shut with a *clop*. 'Please stop bothering to deny it. You must have had contact with your uncle long before you say you did, otherwise you would not be familiar with his room in that wretched boarding house.'

'I was not familiar with them!' she

protested. 'I was there for the first time yesterday!'

'Didn't you tell Inspector Laurie that you came up and knocked on your uncle's door, but it was always bolted and quiet?'

'Yes.'

'How did you know the closed door was *bolted?*' I asked.

'Well, I . . . '

'Miss Usher, there is no way you could have known that had you not been familiar with the door and the room. I suspect you had been in contact with your uncle for quite some time. I also suspect that you donned the coat and hat of a man, managed to get your uncle inebriated, took him to his room, and somehow facilitated his burning. Frankly, I am still not sure how you managed that, but I am willing to listen to you explain it.'

'I do not have to explain anything to you,' she said.

'Arguably so, though I believe I know where your uncle kept his money. You tell me how you killed him, and I will give you my information.'

Gemma Usher gave me a steely gaze, then opened the door and allowed me in. Her house was dark and sparsely furnished. 'Very well,' she said, shutting the door again, 'since you insist upon insinuating yourself into my business, I will tell you.' She went to a nearby table and picked up an unused flower vase. 'My father was a fine and good man, but his brother, my Uncle Robert, was nothing but a wastrel who spent every penny he ever had on his own hedonism. Watching his descent into the gutter broke both of my parents. They died long before they should have. But Uncle Robert kept going on, caring for no one but himself. And then the wretch is rewarded for it by winning the sweepstakes!' She clenched her hands around the vase and I could see fire forming in her eyes. 'My father dies of his worries, and my mother follows him in grief, and yet my worthless uncle becomes rich! It was too much to bear. I decided that he was not fit to live. I would rid the world of him and make proper use of his undeserved reward. You want me to admit it? Very well: yes, I killed him. I thought about how to do it for a long time. I considered many methods.'

As she spoke, she moved the vase in a circular motion, and for the first time I realised there was some kind of liquid in it.

'But then he himself provided me with the method when he happened to mention one of the odious habits he had picked up on the streets. He would measure a length of tallow, light it, put it between his toes, and then fall asleep, awakening when the wick burnt down and the flame touched his flesh. He had some foolish expression for it.'

'Using a candle for a crow,' I said.

'Yes, the flame of the candle acts like the cock-crow dawn, or some such. I find it annoying when the destitute try to excuse their poverty with quaintness, as though a clever metaphor makes their lifestyle acceptable. However, I saw how it could use it to my advantage. I realised that I could kill him in a better way than the one I had been planning. Have you ever read *Bleak House?*'

'Yes,' I uttered.

'Dickens writes of the body so corrupted that it bursts into flame and is consumed,' she went on. 'No one was more corrupted than Robert Usher. What a perfect, poetic way for him to die, and leave no trace of the killing. It was far better than the method I had been considering: vitriol in the face.'

As I gasped, she swirled the liquid in the vase more vigorously.

'The last time I met with Uncle Robert, I managed to get him drunk. It was hardly a challenge, despite all his so-called reformation. But in his last drink, I added a bit of poison. When he began to feel the effects of it, I walked him home: disguised, as you guessed, as a man. At his door, I told him I would be back the first thing the next morning, and demanded he be awake and ready to greet me. I suggested he use his tallow trick. I also encouraged him to bolt his door, and heard him do so. Then I left and waited for the inevitable. The poison did its work, and the alcohol within his body fuelled the eventual fire. At last, my parents were avenged.'

Now I could not take my eyes off of the vase in her grasp, for I had concluded what the liquid was inside it.

'Now,' Gemma Usher continued, 'if you really have information as to the whereabouts of my uncle's money, you had best tell me about it.'

'Would you please put that vase down?' I asked.

'Oh, I would not like to do that,' she said. 'I might burn myself. I believe I asked about my uncle's money.'

'If you kill me you will never know,' I said, straining for an air of calm that I was definitely not feeling.

'I am still waiting.'

I took a deep breath and said: 'This is merely speculation on my part, but my guess is that he had the money on his person. It was burned in the fire.'

Her eyes grew wide, and she stopped swirling the vase. 'No, that cannot be.'

'Why not?' I asked. 'A man who had lived as your uncle had would have become used to keeping his belongings with him at all times, and who would think that such a man would be carrying a vast sum of money? It was the perfect hiding place.'

'You are lying!' she shouted, and suddenly threw the contents of the vase directly towards me. Without even thinking, I dove out of the way and crashed painfully down onto the floor, hearing a hissing sound behind me. When I looked up, I saw that a small wooden table was bubbling and dissolving from the corrosive that had been meant for me! Leaping to my feet, I ran for the door of the house, wrenched it open, and ran straight into the arms of my husband John!

'Amelia!' he cried, looking stunned. 'What are you . . . why . . . what is going on?'

Beside him was an equally surprised-looking Inspector Laurie, flanked by a group of uniformed constables who rushed into the room. 'Be careful!' I shouted. 'She tried to throw vitriol on me!'

'God in heaven!' John declared, wrapping his arms around me. 'Really, my dear, this was too great a chance you took, coming here.'

'A greater chance than I anticipated, darling,' I admitted. 'But how is it that you and Inspector Laurie are here?'

My husband looked down, appearing slightly embarrassed. 'I went straight to the Yard and began to expound upon my theory, but when I got to the part about the victim complaining about his knees, Laurie jumped upon it,' he said. 'What he heard was *my niece*, and immediately began to suspect Miss Usher. We came here to question her, and . . . well, here we are.'

The constables were now leading Gemma Usher out, who glared glacially at me as she passed. Inspector Laurie stopped long enough to say: 'Please, Mrs. Watson, come to me first the next time.' Then he followed his men to the waiting police wagon.

John, meanwhile, was tempering his concern for me with a look of deflation. 'What is wrong, darling?' I asked. 'Are you angry with me?'

'Angry? I should be, over your taking such a chance,' he said. 'But that is not what is bothering me.'

'What then?'

'Amelia, you have solved another case, while I was making a fool of myself yet again. Every time I begin to think of myself as a detective, I do nothing more than reveal my inadequacies.'

'But John, had you not provided the inspector with the key to solving the case, who knows what might have happened? Miss Usher might have got away with two murders, while I . . . oh, I don't even want to think about it.'

'I suppose you are right,' John said, with a rueful smile, 'though it seems exceedingly clear that I shall never be Sherlock Holmes.'

'And thank heaven for that,' I replied, giving him a kiss on the cheek.

The Adventure of the Wrong Watson

'What are you two whispering about?' I demanded of my husband John and our maid, Missy, who were huddled conspiratorially by the fireplace.

'You shouldn't raise your voice, Amelia, not with your throat so sore,' John called back.

'Then for heaven's sake, get over here where I can talk to you in a civil voice.' I sneezed mightily into my handkerchief, and afterwards dabbed the raw edges of my poor nose. Of all the times to catch a cold! Right as John was about to leave on another of his beloved lecture engagements — this one, I believe, was in Wales, though the location hardly mattered. The entire world, it seemed, had an insatiable appetite for the exploits of Sherlock Holmes, as related by his long-time friend and chronicler. Then again, my sudden illness was hardly surprising, given the weather in London. Christmas was but a few weeks away, but instead of the light dusting of holiday snow we had experienced last year, it was cold, rainy and depressingly grey. Coming in from the outside damp and chilled air was no doubt what had given me my ailment.

'What Missy and I were discussing,' John said, stepping over and seating himself beside me on the edge of the chaise longue, 'was her request for this afternoon and evening, and the next two days, off. She would like to visit her sister in Gravesend.'

'But that will leave me here alone,' I protested.

'Which is the best thing for you,' he replied. 'Not to mention us.'

'And what was that intended to mean?'

'It means, Amelia, that you are not on your best behaviour when sick.'

The brute! Here I was, bravely struggling to keep the house running, refusing to give in to a fever that would have felled a dray horse, and receiving nothing but insults in return! 'I will have you know,' I snorted, with justifiable indignation, 'that not only do I not suffer a decline in affability when feeling poorly, I actually mellow into the very soul of patience and grace, in spite of the adversity. And if you are too insensitive to realise it, then may I suggest that you — '

'That I what, dear?' John interrupted.

'That you . . . you . . . oh, heavens.' I slumped against the back of the chaise. 'I was about to say something awful. Perhaps you are right about my mood while ill, John.'

'No one is at their best with a fever,' he said, gently. 'I have done all that I can for you by way of treatment. This fever must simply run its course, and it can do so without us. I recommend that you turn in early tonight and sleep as late as you can tomorrow. Missy will be back before you know it.'

'That's right, mum,' Missy chimed in. 'I'll be back first thing Monday morning.'

'Very well,' I sighed. 'Unless my appetite makes a miraculous recovery, I cannot foresee wanting anything to eat

94

until Monday except some broth, and even if I do recover, I am sure I can scrabble up some food for myself. Have a good time, both of you.'

I must have dozed off on the chaise shortly thereafter, for the next thing I remember is John gently awakening me to tell me that he was about to leave. 'Missy has . . . gone already — ' (Was it my imagination, or had he almost said *fled?*) ' — and I must catch the 4.15 from St Pancras. Just rest and I will see you when I return. Should you have a problem, Dr. Fennyman is on the telephone exchange.'

'Goodbye, darling,' I bade him, punctuating the sentiment with an horrific sneeze.

I tried returning to sleep once he had gone, but the very quiet of our home that afternoon taunted me, and I felt more awake than I had all day. Glancing out the window, I saw nothing but gloom, which did nothing to help my spirits. Rising unsteadily, I made my way to John's desk, where Missy had deposited the morning's post. I slit open the envelopes and began examining the contents. Most of the mail was routine, though there was one letter that immediately stood out from the rest, because at first glance, it appeared to be written in Welsh:

REHTAF SI YLLANIF DAED.
DEDIA YB A PORD FO NOSIOP.
ON ENO NAC ECART TI OT
EM.
ETATSE WON ENIM.
NOOS, EVOL.
G

Who on earth could have sent such a peculiar message? I checked the envelope for the sender's address, but found none. It was then, however, that I saw that the envelope had been addressed to *J. Watson, Quick Street, London*. Clearly, the letter had been delivered to the wrong Watson household, something that neither Missy nor I had noticed. I suppose this is one of the prices of having a spouse whose reputation borders on celebrity that every piece of mail bearing the words 'Watson' and 'London' will now find its way to our home. Since I was in no mood for puzzles, I set the mysterious note aside, mentally vowing to return it to the post office as soon as I was fit enough and let the dead letter office deal with it.

Nothing else in the mail seemed to demand immediate attention, so I rose and started back for the chaise. But halfway there, I stopped, as my previous thought flashed almost visibly through my mind: *Dead letter office.*

Dead.

Despite my bleariness (or perhaps on account of it) I could see the letters of the word, but why? Then it struck me. Returning to the desk I took up the letter once more and reread the first line, *REHTAF SI YLLANIF DAED*, paying particular attention to the last word.

DAED spelled backwards was *DEAD*.

'Good heavens,' I muttered, as I hunted down a pen and began transcribing letters on a clean sheet of paper. The note was not written in Welsh, but rather in perfect English — but it had been painstakingly written backwards. Upon scribbling the last word of the note, I held up the transcription and read:

FATHER IS FINALLY DEAD.
AIDED BY A DROP OF POISON.
NO ONE CAN TRACE IT TO
ME.
ESTATE NOW MINE.
SOON, LOVE.
G

Having felt feverishly hot for the entire afternoon, I now became quite chilled. The note was a virtual confession of complicity in patricide! Clearly, there was only one thing to do: call Inspector Laurie of Scotland Yard. But before I could make it to the telephone — a device that normally I detest, but which does, I must admit, occasionally prove its usefulness — I was interrupted by a knock on the door. 'Missy, would you answer that, please?' I called out, but then I remembered that Missy had gone. Part of me wanted to ignore it, but the knocking seemed insistent, so I stepped into the hall and shuffled down to the front door, sniffling with every step. I opened it and saw a woman whom I guessed to be roughly twenty-five years of age, certainly no more, struggling with an umbrella. She was fashionably dressed, with a fox coat and with a large hat pinned atop her golden hair. She smiled prettily and said: 'I am sorry to disturb you, but does a Dr. J. H. Watson live here?'

I fended off a sneeze long enough to say: 'Yes, but he is not here at the moment. But come in, that weather is miserable.'

She stepped inside and I closed the door behind her, forcing the cold wetness back outside.

'I came by to give Dr. Watson this letter,' the woman said, handing me an envelope. 'It was delivered to us by mistake.'

I took it and read: *Dr. J. H. Watson, 17 Queen Anne Street, London.*

'My husband's name is Watson, too,' she went on, 'Jeremiah Watson, so I suppose the error is understandable, although he is hardly a doctor. My name is Gloria, by the way.'

'Pleased to make your acquaintance,' I

replied. 'I would ask you up, but I'm afraid I am rather ill and would make poor company.'

'I am sorry to hear that. Is someone looking after you?'

'I'm afraid not,' I muttered. 'I am presently alone.'

'Then perhaps I should come in and offer my assistance,' she said.

'No, thank you, I shall be fine,' I moaned. 'I appreciate your returning this.' I reached for the door and started to open it for her, but she pushed against it, closing it. That was strange enough, but for an instant, I thought I saw her sunny face cloud over and turn quite steely. In another second, however, the sun shone again.

'One more thing,' she said. 'I don't suppose you happened to receive any mail that is not yours, have you?' Her smile seemed rather desperate now, and then it struck me: her name was *Gloria* and the sinister letter was signed *G*! Had she written the ominous letter that had been delivered to us by mistake? Could this seemingly delicate young creature really have aided in her own father's death?

'Mrs. Watson . . . it *is* Mrs. Watson, isn't it?' she was saying. 'I was asking if you had received a letter addressed to a J. Watson on Quick Street. You see, Jeremiah has been waiting for an important letter, and having received your letter in error, I was wondering if perhaps the two envelopes did not somehow get switched at the postal office, so that his was delivered here.'

'I have seen no such letter,' I lied. 'If it turns up, I will send it to you. Now, I do not wish to appear rude, but I am feeling very poorly and must get back to my bed. Please understand.' I opened the door again and took her gently by the arm, guiding her out. 'Thank you again. Good day.'

She was still protesting when I closed the door sharply and then latched it. Feeling dizzy, I managed to make my way back to the day room and sat down. *I must contact the police*, I thought hazily. *That girl might be a murderer.* After all, I had what virtually amounted to a letter of confession from her . . . or did I? Could it be that my fevered brain was making more of this than was really there? Before I picked up the telephone and placed a call to Scotland Yard, I had to make sure I was not merely being foolish. I lurched over to the desk and re-examined the letter and envelope. The name and address matched those that she had mentioned, and her own name corresponded to the signature initial of the letter. I then retranslated the backwards writing to ensure that I had not made any errors the first time. I had not. The note definitely described an act of murder-for-inheritance.

Setting down the letter, I felt compelled me to go to the window that faced the street. Perhaps I was hoping for the coincidence of seeing a constable in front of our door, and therefore not have to make a specific call to summon one. Staggering over, my head seemingly filled with liquid, I pulled the curtains back and peered out. I could not see a constable on the grey, rainy street below, but I did see my mysterious visitor, who was standing on the pavement staring at our house, all touches of pleasantness on her face having fallen away, replaced by visible anger and determination! Obviously, my lie regarding the letter had not been convincing.

With a growing sense of fear, I crouched down, so as not to be spotted in the window. After a few seconds, the woman crossed the street and began making a series of odd gestures, all the while keeping her eyes on the house. That she was signalling a confederate was confirmed by the sudden appearance of a man, whose back was turned to the window, making it impossible to see his face. I was, however, able to see Gloria Watson clearly enough to notice her pointing straight to our door!

I was hardly clearheaded, given the agonies wrought by this cold, but one thought fought through to the top of my mind loudly and clearly: calling for help on the telephone would not be sufficient . . . *I must instead get out of this house!*

After throwing on my suit jacket and shoes, I prepared to brave the outdoors — certainly not because I wanted to, but because venturing forth was certainly better than the prospect of being endangered inside my own home. I planned to hail the first cab I saw and instruct them to take me to Scotland Yard as quickly as possible, counting on the assumption that no one would further accost me on a public street.

I opened the door only to be hit in the face with a gust of cold, wet wind. Forcing myself out, I rushed to the kerb to seek out a cab. Naturally, there were none in sight. I had not bothered to bring an umbrella with me, something I now bitterly regretted. I was about to turn and go back inside when I noticed that Gloria Watson was still standing across the street. What was more, she now saw me, and was starting back across the road!

I attempted to run, but after clumsily bumping into a half-dozen other pedestrians, and muttering terse apologies, a sudden realisation brought me to a halt. *I had not thought to bring the letter with me!* Even if I did reach the inspector's office in one piece, what evidence of my claim would I have to show him? It was at that point that another concern overtook me: *Had I remembered to lock the front door behind me?* For if I had not, it was a virtual invitation for the woman — or the man who was her confederate — to enter our home, conduct a search, and possibly stay there awaiting my return.

What should I do? I demanded of myself, but my head felt like the tides were rushing back and forth inside it, making rational thought elusive, if not impossible. Out of utter frustration, I stamped my foot on the pavement — a fit of pique that unfortunately served to break the heel of my left shoe, causing me to lose my balance on the wet stone and fall down hard. I cried out, more from discomfiture than actual pain, and saw that a crowd of people was forming around me, taking in the spectacle I was making of myself. Any moment now I expected to see the form of Gloria Watson looming over me.

Instead, however, to my intense relief, I saw a police constable working his way through the crowd. 'Madam, are you incapacitated?' he asked.

I began coughing violently and suddenly felt quite dizzy. 'I live less than a street away,' I moaned, 'do you suppose you could help me home?'

'Yes'm,' he agreed, helping me up. Before long I felt another set of hands on me.

'Is there a problem here?' asked a young man with a sporty moustache, who was now supporting me on the other side. 'May I be of help? I'm a doctor. My name is Simons.'

'A good thing you came along, sir,' the constable replied. 'The lady has taken a fall, and she appears to be ill. Her home is this way; would you mind helping me, sir?'

'Not at all,' Dr. Simons said, practically picking me up and carrying me down the street to my front door — which, I grimly noted, I had forgotten to lock behind me. But no matter, an officer of the police was now here. Once inside, the two took me up to the day room and set me down on the chaise longue.

'Let me get you something to drink, Mrs . . . ' the doctor said, heading straight for the small drinks cabinet John keeps near his desk.

'Watson,' I replied, hoarsely. 'Mrs. John Watson, and just some water will be fine.'

'If you're all right now, madam, I'll be off,' the constable said.

'Please don't leave yet,' I entreated. 'I'm afraid that someone will try to harm me.'

Just then Dr. Simons came back with a glass of water. 'What's this about someone trying to harm you?' he asked.

I sipped from the glass and then attempted to explain the bizarre occurrences that had taken place this afternoon, but listening to my own words as they feverishly tumbled out, even I was becoming confused. 'Constable,' I said, finally, 'go and see the note for yourself. It's on the table over there, along with my translation.'

He sauntered over and examined the tabletop, but then turned to me a moment later, frowning. 'I'm sorry, madam, but there are no letters here.'

I attempted to leap off the chaise, but the best I could manage was a woozy, unsteady rise. 'Then someone has been here already!' I cried, following the expulsion of breath with a racking cough, and settling back down. 'They have taken the note with them!' An even more frightening thought then struck me. 'Constable, what if they are still here in the house, hiding somewhere?'

The constable exchanged a quick glance with Dr. Simons, then said: 'I suppose it wouldn't hurt to investigate.' With the doctor in tow, he carefully looked through every room, every closet, and even behind some of the furniture, before concluding: 'If someone is hiding in here, madam, they must be the size of Tom Thumb. Now then, tell us again about this woman who came to see you.'

'Her name was Gloria Watson.'

'And it was she who signed that missing letter?'

'There was no signature on the note, only the initial 'G', but Gloria Watson visited me earlier today and asked for the note back.'

'And she admitted to writing the letter?'

'Well, actually no, but who else could have written it? She certainly knew about it.'

'Did she say anything about the contents of the letter?'

'Well . . . no.'

'So there is nothing that actually connects her with the implication in the letter that someone's father has been killed.'

'She did not have to!' I cried, irritably. 'The letter was addressed to J. Watson and signed by someone whose initial began with G. The woman's name is Gloria, and her husband is Jeremiah Watson. She knew about the letter and suspected that I had it. Isn't that enough, Constable?'

'It might be, if you actually had the letter,' he replied. 'You see, madam, all I have to go on now is your word that there really was a letter and there really was a woman.'

'Of *course* there was a letter and of *course* there was a woman, and — ' My head began to throb again. 'Oh, I must get out of this wet dress and lie down,' I moaned.

'Pardon me for saying so, Mrs. Watson, but you do not look well at all,' Dr. Simons said. 'I would be happy to accompany you to the hospital.'

'Oh, no, no, I shall be all right if I rest.'

'Perhaps I should summon a doctor for you?'

'Yes, please contact Dr. Fennyman, if you would,' I replied. 'He is on the telephone exchange.'

'Oh, I know Fennyman,' Dr. Simons said, bustling to the telephone, 'I'll get him at once.'

Closing my sore and tired eyes, I heard him signal the exchange, wait, and then say: 'Dr. Fennyman? This is Dr. Simons. Fine, thank you. I'm at the home of Mrs. Watson in Queen Anne Street, and there appears to be a problem. I don't have my bag with me, so could you come over? This afternoon? Fine. Goodbye.' Walking back to the chaise, he announced: 'He should be here within the hour. He recommended that you rest until then.'

'An excellent idea,' the constable said, with a patronising smile.

'You don't believe anything I've told

you, do you?' I asked, miserably.

'Well, madam, I'd feel better if I could see that letter for myself. But in the meantime, I'll do some checking and see if anyone has reported the death of a man who can be traced to a woman named Gloria Watson. That's the best I can do. Now then, I really must be going.'

'As must I,' Dr. Simons echoed. 'It would perhaps be best, Mrs. Watson, if you followed us out and locked the door behind us, if you are up to it.'

'I will manage,' I said, getting up and staggering to the front door behind them and throwing the latch after they had gone. 'Oh, maybe they are right,' I moaned, as I dragged myself back to the day room. 'Maybe I am making too much of this.'

I doffed my damp clothes and put on a nightdress, then made myself a cup of tea and lay back on the chaise, listening to the patter of the raindrops. No sooner had I reclined than I promptly fell asleep, only to awaken at dusk in the throes of a coughing fit and a pounding in my head. I looked at the clock — it was half-past eight, and chilly, since the fire in the hearth had burnt itself out. Where was Dr. Fennyman? I then realised that the pounding was not in my head, but coming from the front door. Surely it must be he.

'Missy, the door!' I croaked, but then realised my foolish error. The girl was still out. I would have to answer it myself. Rising, I dragged my aching body to the door and swung it open. 'Thank you for finally coming,' I said, 'please come in, Doctor . . . oh, Dr. Simons, it's you.'

'I came by to check on you,' the young physician said, stepping inside. 'Has Fennyman been by?'

'Not unless I slept through his knock,' I replied, with a cough.

'Gads, what can the man be doing?' he exclaimed. 'Let me go up and call him again for you.' As he began to ascend the stair, I looked out onto the street and noticed a cab stopped in front of the house. Inside the cab I clearly saw Gloria Watson, glaring at me like a malignant spectre!

Slamming the door, I cried, 'Call the

police immediately!' Pulling myself back up the stairs as quickly as I could, I lurched back into the day room.

Dr. Simons was already speaking on the telephone. 'What's wrong?' he asked me.

'That woman, she's outside the front, waiting,' I gasped. 'Please telephone the police.'

'Fennyman, I have to go,' he said, and while he re-signalled the exchange operator, I lurched over to John's desk and pulled out the second drawer, looking for his service revolver. It was nowhere to be found.

'This is an emergency!' Dr. Simons barked into the telephone. 'Come at once! Yes, yes, I'll wait.' After ringing off, he asked: 'Mrs. Watson, did you lock the front door after you let me in?'

I froze. 'I cannot recall,' I whispered.

'Stay here,' he commanded, leaving the room. After a minute of cold silence, I called his name, but received no answer. Had he gone outside? I was about to call again when I heard a sharp cry. 'Doctor!' I shouted hoarsely, and stepped out into the hall.

Had my throat been capable of issuing a scream, I no doubt would have done so at the sight that greeted me at the bottom of the stairs: Dr. Simons was sprawled across the floor, while Gloria Watson stood over him with a knife in her hand! Then she turned and looked up at me with a malicious smile.

I rushed back inside, but my growing panic, combined with another sudden spell of dizziness, conspired against me. I got no further than the dining room before I fell to the floor. I managed to climb into a chair, and watched helplessly as Gloria Watson steadily approached me, the knife still clutched in her hand.

'Is he dead?' I croaked.

'What do you think?' she answered.

'What are you going to do with me?'

'Surely you understand that I cannot allow you to live,' she said, pulling from her pocket a sheet of paper that I recognised as my translation of her letter. 'It was careless of me to put such a message in writing, but what's done is done. I cannot change it now. All I can do now is protect myself.' She stepped closer.

'The police will be here any moment,' I said, managing to muster up an ounce of defiance. 'Dr. Simons telephoned them.'

'Did he?' she asked, now close enough to reach out and touch me.

At that instant I saw a shadow against the wall behind her, and focusing on it, realised that Dr. Simons was standing in the doorway — he was not dead!

'Doctor, do something!' I cried, but he made no move. When I saw his smile, the horrid truth dawned upon me and I realised that I had been a complete fool. He produced a pistol, walked slowly to the woman and handed it to her.

'Actually my name is Jeremiah Watson,' he said, 'though it is quite amazing how quickly you can insinuate yourself into a household by claiming to be a doctor. I must try it again sometime. And I'm afraid you were right, Gloria, that death scene I had so carefully devised did not work.'

'I knew it wouldn't,' she replied, sliding the knife under her belt. Then to me she said: 'You see, Mrs. Watson, Jerry presumed that the sight of an apparent murder would cause you to faint, which would make killing you much easier and cleaner. I tried to tell him that not every woman could be counted on to swoon in the face of something unpleasant.'

'How wise of you,' I groaned. 'To think, all this time I was worried about a break-in, and it was really your husband who stole the letter right out from under the noses of the constable and myself, while pretending to call Dr. Fennyman and the police. And I assume it was him that I saw you speaking with on the street.'

'It was,' she replied, 'though we are not married yet. It was easier to tell you that we were — and we will be, as soon as Father's will clears probate and I take possession of the Pembroke estate.'

Another part of the deadly note became clear: *SOON, LOVE*. 'So . . . Miss Pembroke, is it? You killed your own father for his money,' I said, talking while my mind desperately searched for a means of escape.

'No, not for money,' she replied, bitterly, 'for my *life*! My father controlled every aspect of my life, right down to the people I associated with. He did not approve of Jerry, or anyone else that I liked. He threatened to disown me if the marriage went through. He had a heart condition, and had already outlived his doctors' expectations. I merely hastened the inevitable, and in doing so, regained my life. You no doubt think me heartless, but I am not. I will not particularly enjoy having to kill you, but I have no choice. Blame the Royal Mail if you like. If not for their mix-up, you would live to see the morning.'

As she raised the gun, I shut my eyes and began to pray. At times, I have wondered about what my last thought, word or action on earth would be, and now that the time had come, I realised to my chagrin that my last official act among the living would be trying not to sneeze.

But then, as I silently thought of John and prepared for the end, a knock came at the door! Opening my eyes, I saw Jeremiah run to the window and peer out.

'It's that blasted constable!'

'Don't answer it,' Miss Pembroke commanded.

'But what if he gets suspicious?' the man hissed.

'All right, open it, but take her with you,' she commanded. To me, she said: 'You tell him everything is fine and get rid of him.' Then, handing the gun back to her fiancé, she said: 'Keep the gun on her, and if there is any trouble, shoot both of them.'

Positioning me in front of him, while keeping the gun pressed against my back, Jeremiah Watson marched me out of the front door, which I opened. 'Good evening, Constable,' I managed to mutter.

'Evening, madam,' he responded. 'Oh, hello, Doctor, I didn't realise you had come back.'

'Yes, I told Mrs. Watson that I would stop in and see how she was doing, which appears to be much better.'

'I see, sir. Well, madam, I wanted to tell you that we've hit a brick wall with that name you gave us, Gloria Watson. If you happen to come up with any other information — '

'As a matter of fact, I already have,' I said, quickly. 'There's a man involved, and his name is . . . ' I could feel the gun barrel digging into my back. ' . . . Robert Laurie. You must find him immediately.'

'Robert Laurie?' the constable said. 'But that's — '

'A Scottish name, yes, I know. But it is up to you, Constable. You must find Robert Laurie at once.'

'Very well,' the policeman muttered.

'Oh, dear,' I moaned, slumping back against Jeremiah Watson, 'I fear I've overdone it again. Thank you for stopping by, Constable. Dr. Simons, please help me back inside.'

'Yes, of course,' Jeremiah said. 'Good night, Constable. And don't worry, I'll see that she's taken care of.'

After the door was closed and locked, Jeremiah asked: 'What was that business about Robert Laurie?'

'It is just a name to throw them off the track,' I replied. 'Would you rather I had said Jeremiah Watson?'

119

'You would not still be alive if you had.'

After depositing me back on the chaise, Jeremiah Watson handed the gun back to his fiancé.

'Has the policeman gone?' Gloria asked.

'Yes,' he answered. 'At least, I think he has. But perhaps we should wait for a bit, to make sure.'

'All right,' she agreed. 'That will also give us an opportunity to prepare our stories.'

As they talked, an eternity seemed to be passing by. But after only three-quarters of an hour, the woman said: 'He's not coming back. Let's get it over with.' Raising the gun to my chest, she began to count: 'One, two . . . '

'No, wait!' I cried. 'Please, not here.'

'Now what?' Jeremiah Watson shouted nervously.

'I realise there is no way I can save myself, but please, take me somewhere else,' I said. 'Tie me up first, blindfold me, do whatever you wish, I no longer care. But do not kill me here. I do not want my husband to come home to the sight of my dead body in our own home. You said, Miss Pembroke, that you were not a heartless person. This is your chance to prove it.'

'This is some kind of trick,' Jeremiah said.

'No, she's right,' the woman responded. 'It would be better if her body was found elsewhere. Or never found at all.' The expression on her face indicated that she was thinking the matter over. 'All right, we'll take her. I'll go out and flag a cab, and then give you a signal. I'll throw a stone against the window. When you hear that, bring her outside, and we'll work out where to go from there. And please don't consider trying to escape, Mrs. Watson.' I didn't bother telling her that, given my physical condition at present, which found me struggling even to stay conscious, I could no more have escaped than I could have danced an Irish jig on my hands.

Seconds after Gloria left the room, we heard the front door open and close. An agonisingly long minute after that came the clattering of a pebble against the glass. 'That's the signal,' Jeremiah said, 'come on.'

'At least let me get a wrap,' I said.

'Hurry it up, and don't attempt anything foolish.'

After throwing my squirrel coat overtop my nightdress, we went out into the cool night to find a largely deserted street.

'Where's the cab?' Jeremiah asked.

From directly behind us, another voice said: 'You'll be going in a different vehicle, sir.' And in a flash, a half-dozen constables were on top of the man, wresting the pistol from his hand, while I was cast off into the arms of another policeman. Two others held the angry, struggling figure of the blonde woman.

'Are you all right Mrs. Watson?' a voice asked, and I turned to see Inspector Robert Laurie, with whom I had been thrust into several peculiar adventures that my husband would have termed *cases*.

'I have been better,' I coughed.

As a police four-wheeler was arriving to take away the criminals, I made it a point to seek out and thank the constable whose acquaintance I had made earlier in the day, and who had had enough wits about him to understand my message.

'Well, madam,' said the policeman, who was finally introduced to me as PC Turley, 'your message was clear enough, asking for the inspector and all, but I might not have followed through if it wasn't for the look of desperation in your eyes.'

Once he was finished directing the capture, Inspector Laurie sauntered over to my side. 'Someday, Mrs. Watson,' he said, a wry smile gracing his usually sombre face, 'you must tell me how you manage to find trouble so consistently.'

I was about to reply, but all of a sudden my illness and the events of the day all caught up with me at once, and I felt myself sinking to the ground in what was later described to me as a dead faint.

The Adventure of the Haunted Wager

I was pinning on my hat, preparing to go out to the flower market at Covent Garden, when a knock came at the door. As I was not expecting anybody, I assumed it was for my husband John, who was, alas, not home, but was instead spending a rare morning away from his writing desk to actually put in time at his surgery. 'Please get that, Missy,' I called to our maid.

The girl returned a moment later and said, under her breath: 'Mum, that strange little man of yours is here to see you.'

'Strange little man of mine?' I repeated, and then broke out into a laugh as I realised she must mean Harry Benbow. Sure enough, Harry danced his way into our day room a few seconds later.

'Hello, ducks!' Harry cried happily, doffing his battered bowler hat.

'Hello, Harry,' I replied, already smiling. Missy, on the other hand, was staring at the little man as though he had just come down from another planet. When Harry noticed her stern-faced reaction to him, he executed a broad, theatrical 'take', and stopped dancing. Then he affected a remarkably accurate facsimile of her puzzled expression, turning to me and shrugging his shoulders. By now I was nearly helpless with laughter. 'That will . . . be all . . . Missy,' I managed to gasp out, and the girl gave a bobbing curtsey, turned, and walked away, looking more befuddled than ever.

When she had gone, Harry said, 'Gettin' a grin out of that 'un is like tryin' to squeeze a pint out of a carrot.'

'You certainly appear to be in a good mood, Harry,' I said.

'That I am, ducks,' he said, his grin practically meeting behind his ears. 'Fact is, I came over here today to ask if you'd do the honour of havin' lunch with me today — my treat.'

'Lunch, Harry? Well, I — '

'Oh, I know what you're thinkin',' he interrupted. 'Poor ol' Harry ain't got two farthings to clink together, so how can he take anyone to lunch?'

'Well . . . '

'No need to hedge, Amelia. I'm the first one to admit that in the past couple o' years, I ain't been livin' up to the earnin' potential of me youth. But all that's about to change. I'll tell you all about it at lunch. I got the place all picked out.'

The place turned out to be a rather dark and pungent fish shop near Euston Station, Harry's most recent place of employment. Still, his company brightened up even the dankest surroundings. 'So, Harry, tell me about this new opportunity for you,' I said.

'Better yet, my girl, I'll show it to you,' Harry replied, pulling a creased piece of newsprint from his jacket pocket, which he set down on the table and carefully smoothed out. There was nothing on the page that drew my attention in particular, until he pointed to a small boxed advertisement which read:

'What does this mean, Harry?' I asked.

'It means ducks, that I'll soon be in the chips! I'm going to earn enough bees-and-honey to pay for this lunch a hundred times over! And all I have to do is spend a night in a haunted house.'

'You must be joking, Harry.'

'Not a bit of it. See, there's these two blokes, and one of 'em — Gillingwater, his name is — makes a livin' claimin' to talk to the spirit world. He does séances, table rappings, you name it. You oughta hear him rabbit on about it . . . ' Harry suddenly transformed himself in manner

127

and voice into an ethereal seeker of mysteries, and even though I had never met Mr. Gillingwater, I knew Harry's talents well enough to accept that it was an accurate impersonation. The appearance of a serving girl bearing two plates of steaming fish and chips, however, resulted in Harry suddenly snapping back to himself.

'Ah, here we go!' he said, his eyes growing wide in anticipation of the meal, over which he poured at least a half-pint of malt vinegar before tucking in with vigour. I approached the fish much more tentatively, but was pleasantly surprised by its flavour, which was far better than I had expected.

'Anyway,' Harry went on, delicately retrieving a slender bone from his teeth, 'the other cove, Cardew, is just the opposite. He don't believe in anythin' what he can't see, touch or taste, and he's out to prove that Gillingwater an' his ilk are nothin' but cheats. He used to be a stage conjuror, so he knows all the tricks they use.'

'And they have hired you to spend a

night in a haunted house?'

'That's right. The two of them have a bet with each other. If a third party, not connected with either of them — in this case, me — dosses in the place for a night and sees somethin' goin' bump in the night, then Devlin has to pay Gillingwater a thousand pounds. If absolutely nothin' happens — no floatin' shapes, no clankin' chains, no moans — then Gillingwater hands over the same amount. An' the beauty of it is, no matter what happens I get a hundred quid for my trouble.'

'And you're certain that the loser will accept your testimony without question?' I asked.

'They've both agreed to take what I say as gospel. Though from what I've seen of Mr. Cardew, he'd as soon believe in flyin' cows before acceptin' the possibility that he could be wrong.'

'What happens if you see something you cannot explain and Mr. Cardew refuses to believe you?'

'I have their word, ducks, the word of gentlemen. And you know what? Cardew told me they'd interviewed a couple o' dozen blokes for the job, and I had the most honest face o' the lot.'

I could only imagine *the lot*. 'When is your night in the haunted house to take place?'

'Tomorrow night. And I know ducks, that you're always worryin' about me, and I appreciate it, I really do. But trust me, Amelia, this is going to be the easiest money ol' Harry ever made!'

As I nibbled my fish, I regarded Harry with a sculpted smile, genuinely wishing that he had indeed found a bit of good luck, yet feeling deep down inside that this escapade of his was going to turn out as disastrous as all his previous ones.

Alas, how right I was.

Two days after my lunch with Harry, John was perusing *The Times* before heading off for an appointment with his publisher. As he focused on one particular page, I saw his handsome face darken. 'Amelia,' he said, 'isn't that music hall chap of yours named Harry Benbow?'

'Yes, why?'

'It appears he has got himself arrested.'

'Oh, heavens, now what?'

'According to the newspaper, he's accused of murdering two men.'

I rushed towards John, rather indelicately wrenched the newspaper out of his hands, and read how Harry had been arrested by the police yesterday morning shortly after he ran outside an empty house in Camden Town — empty, except for the bodies of James Gillingwater and Devlin Cardew, both of whom had been stabbed. Being familiar as I am with Harry's absolute genius for getting himself into trouble, it almost goes without saying that at the time of his apprehension he was clutching the murder weapon, a blood-stained dagger.

'We must contact the police,' I said to John. 'I know Harry had nothing to do with these horrible crimes.'

John sighed. 'Amelia, we cannot get involved with a police investigation of this magnitude.'

'Why not? You and Mr. Holmes have insinuated yourselves into dozens of police cases.'

'No, Amelia, we did not *insinuate ourselves*. On every police case in which

Holmes and I were involved, we had been consulted by the Yard.'

'Fine,' I snapped. 'This newspaper account should provide the name of the investigating inspector, so all there is for it is to present ourselves and demand that we be consulted.'

John sighed again, and I chose to ignore him. 'Here it is,' I said, having scanned down the columns of the news account, 'it says Inspector Stradlee will be conducting the investigation. Are you familiar with him?'

'Quite,' John said, 'and if you expect cooperation of any kind from Stradlee, you had best give him a false name. He and I have . . . well, let us simply say that we have had our differences.'

'Really? Darling, you positively shock me. I thought the world loved you. But no matter: I can explain what I know about Harry to our friend Inspector Laurie, and he can pass it along to this other fellow.'

John sighed yet again — a newfound habit that I was finding rather annoying. 'Very well, but please refrain from *insinuating yourself* into an active investigation.'

He went off to his meeting while I took an omnibus to New Scotland Yard, through which I wended my way with familiarity. Odd as it might seem for the wife of a respectable city doctor, I knew my way around the police headquarters quite well, and many of the officers within the building recognised me at sight. Upon arriving at the office of Inspector Robert Laurie, I found him standing by the door as though waiting for me, a smile on his face.

'I rather thought you might come by, Mrs. Watson,' he said.

'Oh?'

'Yes, I heard about Benbow's arrest, and thought the name sounded familiar. Then I recalled that he was the little chap who had been brought in for the kidnapping of those two boys a year or so back, and that you were the one who helped to clear him.'

'Yes,' I said, remembering the case. 'That was a misunderstanding, and so is this murder business.' I proceeded to tell

Inspector Laurie what Harry had presented to me at lunch two days previously.

'All well and good, Mrs. Watson, but I'm not in charge of the investigation. However, if you like, I'll take you down to Stradlee's office. He is the one with whom you need to speak, though I would not mention that you are married to the doctor if I were you.'

'John mentioned that there was bad blood between him and the inspector,' I said. 'Do you know what that is about?'

'Hasn't he told you?'

'No, he was quite cryptic about it, which for John is astounding.' My husband's ability to keep a secret was roughly equal to that of a cat's to play the hornpipe and dance.

'Let's just say that Stradlee continues to be upset over something your husband has written. On the other hand, he never writes about me at all,' Inspector Laurie added, sounding almost disappointed. 'Anyway, isn't your maiden name something like *petit four*?'

'Pettigrew,' I corrected.

'Right. I will introduce you to Stradlee as Mrs. Pettigrew, and then you can talk to him without cause for concern.'

He led me down the hallway until we came to another office, even more cluttered and scattered than Inspector Laurie's, where a small, ferret-like man was burrowing through stacks of paperwork. Glancing up, he said, 'Yes, what is it?'

'George, this is Mrs. Pettigrew,' Inspector Laurie said, indicating me. 'She's come forth as a witness in that double murder case.'

'She has, has she?' Inspector Stradlee said.

'I suppose you could say she's a character witness for the prime suspect.'

'Ha!' the ferrety policeman barked. 'That's rich! A character witness for Benbow!'

'If you will hear me out, Inspector, I think I can convince you that Harry could not have committed those vile killings.'

'Mm-hmm,' the inspector replied, still searching through the papers on his desk like a large rodent sniffing out food.

'I'll leave you here, Mrs., er, Pettigrew,' Inspector Laurie said, turning to leave.

I stood in the office for a few awkwardly silent moments, then Inspector Stradlee said: 'Go on, then, talk. I'm listening.'

Carefully, I detailed the lunch I had spent with Harry just prior to the murders, repeating what he had told me about the strange wager and the two men who had instigated it, taking special care to describe Harry's almost childlike glee at the opportunity to earn a hundred pounds. 'Surely you can see, Inspector, that there is no earthly reason Harry Benbow would want to kill the men who were about to deliver such a windfall into his hands.'

'Oh, isn't there?' Inspector Stradlee said quickly, focusing his dark eyes on me. 'Well, madam, maybe your friend decided he wasn't quite happy with a hundred pounds. Maybe he wanted two thousand.'

'Two thousand?'

'Just so. Benbow has already told us all about this so-called bet. He says he stayed

136

all night in this old, dark house, listening to nothing but mice scurrying in the walls, seeing nothing but cobwebs blown by draughts, and finally he fell asleep — which wasn't surprising, given how much brandy he'd consumed.'

'Brandy?' I said. 'I've never known Harry to be a heavy imbiber of brandy.'

'There was a near-empty bottle on him,' the inspector said. 'Maybe it was to fortify himself for the night ahead, or maybe you don't know him as well as you think you do. At any rate, when he finally woke up then next morning, there, in the parlour of the house, lay the bodies of Gillingwater and Devlin: both stabbed to death, and the knife that did it lying between them. Benbow claims that he doesn't know when they got there or who did the killing. He also claims that he picked up the knife and ran out of sheer panic. But I know different.'

'You do?' I asked, starting to feel a bit ill.

'Right. The way I see it, Benbow spends the night there, and then waits for the two of them to show up the next morning. He lets them in, stabs them both, and then takes a thousand pounds off each of them, which he knows they're going to be carrying. So instead of a hundred, he's got two thousand. His only mistake was trying to leave through the front door, with the knife in his hand, and getting spotted by one of our men.'

'So, you believe that Mr. Gillingwater and Mr. Cardew showed up in the morning, and that Harry stabbed them when they came in?'

'That's right.'

'How do you stab two men at once, Inspector?'

'Well . . . I don't rightly know, never having done it. Maybe he stabbed one and then the other.'

'While the other calmly stood by and waited for his turn?'

'Well . . . ' His small eyes narrowed, then suddenly widened, as though forced open by an idea. 'I know: he lured one away from the other, stabbed him, then went back for the other.'

'I thought you said they were both found together in the same room?'

'Well . . . he could have moved one of them.'

'Was there any sign of the body being moved?' I asked. 'A trail of blood, perhaps, or a disruption of dust on the floor?'

The ferrety man stood up. 'Look, madam, I agreed to listen to your testimony, which I have. But I'm not about to sit here and be lectured to by someone pretending to be Sherlock Holmes!'

'I am simply trying to help my friend,' I protested.

'Well, the way I see it, nobody can do that. We've got Benbow red-handed. If he didn't kill those two, then it had to be the work of a ghost — and I don't believe in ghosts! Now, good day.'

Realising the futility of attempting to argue further, I started to leave, but then turned back. 'One other thing, Inspector, if you don't mind. When you caught Harry, did he have the two thousand pounds on him?'

'What? No, he didn't.' He then frowned, as though struck by a sudden thought. 'No . . . he didn't. He must have hidden it somewhere in the house.'

'That, or the ghost picked his pocket. Good day, Inspector.'

'Hmmph,' he muttered, waving me off. But before I could get out of the office doorway, a uniformed constable ran up, shouting, 'Inspector Stradlee!' in an alarmed voice.

I stood out of sight just past the door and heard the inspector say, 'What is it?'

'Sir, that murder in Camden Town?' the constable panted. 'We have a problem with one of the bodies.'

'What's the trouble? Spit it out, man.'

'Well sir, it seems the body of Cardew has . . . has disappeared.'

There was a heavy pause before the inspector roared, '*Disappeared?*'

'Yes, sir,' the PC said. 'From the morgue.'

'Oh, for . . . '

I turned away so as not to be noticed by Inspector Stradlee, who charged out of his office with the frightened constable in tow. At least Harry's troubles would not be compounded by the accusation that he stole the body of Mr. Cardew, since he was conveniently — if not comfortably — in custody at the time.

'Excuse me, madam,' a voice said behind me, and I turned to see yet another policeman, a sergeant. 'Can I help you?' he asked.

'Oh, well, I was speaking with Inspector Stradlee, who was unexpectedly called away. I am certain he will be back momentarily. I was hoping to wait for him in his office, if that is permissible.' In truth, I had no intention of waiting for the man, but a thought had come into my mind of what I could do during his absence.

'Right, madam, go ahead,' the sergeant said, then stepped away.

Slipping back inside the office, I looked around the inspector's overcrowded desk until I found a folder labelled 'Camden Town Murders'. Making certain that no one was observing me, I opened the folder and peeped inside, scanning a series of notes written in two different handwritings. One was clearly the testimony of the officer who had arrested

Harry at the site, and the other was the record of a conversation with a Mr. William Bliss, who was identified as Mr. Cardew's business manager, and who had been called in to formally identify his body in lieu of family. According to the notes, Mr. Bliss maintained an office in Fleet Street. There was little else of value in the file, and I was in the act of replacing it the way I had found it when I was interrupted by a cough. Looking up, startled, I saw Inspector Laurie standing in the doorway, a wry smile on his lips.

'Snooping, are we, Mrs. Watson?' he asked.

'Peckish is what we are,' I replied sweetly. 'I don't suppose you have time in your busy schedule for tea, do you?'

Minutes later we were seated in a small tea shop in Whitehall Court. 'The body disappeared, you say?' Inspector Laurie exclaimed. 'That is certainly a first. What did Stradlee say about it?'

'He took the news rather badly,' I said, spooning blackberry jam onto a scone. 'What I do not understand is why on earth anyone would want to steal a body.'

'Perhaps there was some incriminating evidence on the body that indicated the man had not been killed the way we think he had, and the real killer — assuming it is not Benbow — had to dispose of the corpse before it could be discovered. Frankly, Mrs. Watson, *why* is not as puzzling as *how*. *How* could someone have got into the police morgue and removed the body without being seen?'

'Could someone have obtained permission to remove it?'

'Yes, all bodies are released eventually, usually to the family, though doing so without the permission or even the knowledge of the investigating officer is quite unheard of.'

'According to the paperwork I just, er, happened to see on Inspector Stradlee's desk, Devlin Cardew had no family,' I said. 'I wonder if William Bliss could have claimed the body. We should check at once.'

'Mrs. Watson, please let me remind you that I am not on this case. What's more, neither are you.'

'You cannot expect me to sit idly back

and watch Harry pay for a crime I know he did not commit.'

Inspector Laurie sighed. (The entire of London, it seemed, was succumbing to sighing sickness.) 'Officially, I can do nothing to undermine Stradlee's authority over this case,' he said. 'Neither can I condone any action by you. More importantly, I cannot necessarily protect you should you take any action that lands you in trouble. But I have known you long enough to realise that I cannot stop you, either. There is, therefore, only one thing I can do.'

'What's that?' I asked.

'Pray that you know what you're doing.'

After tea, the inspector returned to the Yard and I made my way to the Fleet Street offices of William Bliss, which proved to be so much wasted effort since the building was closed up and appeared to be deserted. Had Mr. Bliss vanished as well?

I had no choice but to return home and try to formulate some other plan to help Harry. On the way to Queen Anne Street, however, fate intervened. I happened to pass a small bookseller's shop in Broad Street and, as was my habit when passing a book stall, I glanced over to the window. There, next to a hastily scribbled sign promoting it, was a copy of a tome titled *My Life in Adventure and Truth* by Devlin Cardew. I rushed into the shop to examine the book (which was covered with so much dust that it must have been unearthed from the stacks somewhere in the back and set out to take advantage of the newspaper headlines), and ended up purchasing it.

By the time I got back home John had already returned from his meeting with his publisher, and the evening edition of *The Times* was there as well. The double murders were still fresh on the front page, though there was no mention of the disappearance of Devlin Cardew's body.

'I am hardly surprised that Stradlee refused to offer that fact to the press,' John said, as I related the bizarre occurrence to him. 'In fact, if he knew I was aware of it, he would be likely to explode like a Chinese rocket.'

'What is it between the two of you?' I asked.

'Oh, I've used him as a character in a few stories, is all, and he did not like the way he was depicted.'

'I don't recall ever reading his name in one of your works.'

'I changed his name, but he was able to see through it, and he's convinced everyone else can as well. He believes I have portrayed him as a fool, which is something I cannot help, since in comparison to Holmes he sometimes appears so.'

After making a mental note to reread some of John's stories, I took up the book I had purchased, retreated to the chaise longue by the window, and began to flip through it. Even a perfunctory glance proved that Devlin Cardew was no writer — the text was turgid and repetitive — though he was clearly enamoured of the book's subject: himself. A series of photographic plates showed him in one exotic location after another, from a jungle in Africa to a snowy mountain peak in Tibet. It was another illustration, however, that caught my attention: the reproduction of a poster showing Devlin (a.k.a. 'The Great Cardini') resting in a coffin, under the heading 'Mastery over Death!'. The sheer irony of it caused me to shake my head. With tired eyes, I set the book down and prepared for dinner, thinking no more about it afterwards.

The next morning, with no better ideas, I decided to try once more to rouse William Bliss. Treating myself to a cab to Fleet Street, I was soon at the door of his establishment, which I found once again locked. I knocked several times, more insistently than before, and was just about to give up when the door was suddenly opened by a distinguished-looking grey-haired man. 'We are closed,' he said, brusquely. 'Come back later.'

'Are you Mr. Bliss?' I asked.

'Yes, yes, but the office is closed. Please remove yourself.'

'Mr. Bliss, if I could just come in and talk to you for a moment — ' I began.

'No!' he shouted. 'I mean, I'm sorry, but you cannot come in just now.'

It was almost as though he was hiding

something behind the door that he did not want me to see. 'I need to speak with you about Mr. Cardew,' I insisted.

'Not now, I cannot talk to you now.'

'You have talked to the police, I trust?'

'I talked to them two days ago, not that it is any business of yours. I do not wish to be rude, but you are interrupting — '

'Then you know about the body's disappearance.'

'Yes, yes, it is shocking. Now, really, I must go. Come back tomorrow.'

'Very well,' I said, and the door slammed in front of me. I smiled as I turned to walk away, for I had strengthened my suspicions that William Bliss had removed the body of Devlin Cardew from the police morgue and was evidently concealing it in his office — but for what purpose? I rushed home and relayed this information to John — who, being John, immediately began to puncture holes in my logic.

'What proof have you for this supposition?' he asked. 'Did you see an evidence of a body in Bliss's office?'

'No, I did not, but Mr. Bliss said he

talked to the police two days ago, apparently when he was asked to identify the body. Yet he knew that the body had disappeared, which happened only yesterday, and which was not reported in the newspapers. How could he have known about the disappearance if he had not taken the body himself?'

John stroked his moustache and nodded. 'He could have talked to them since, I suppose, but . . . very well, Amelia, your deductive reasoning is sound. Still, why would he do such a thing?'

'I don't know, darling, I just . . . I just *feel* that I am right. Call it women's intuition if you must.'

John sighed, the brute. 'That is the sort of statement that would make Holmes cringe,' he said. 'However, I know that your intuition has triumphed in the past.'

'As, I have little doubt, has that of Mr. Holmes on occasion, only he will not admit it.'

John smiled. 'Maybe so. He did once remark that the Lama chap from whom he learned his death trick was the most intuitive man he had ever met.'

'Death trick? John, what are you talking about?'

'Holmes spent a few years in Tibet, and during that time the high lama, or yogi, or whatever he was, taught him how to relax his heartbeat and respiration to the point where he appeared to be dead. He did it for me once, and I have to say, it was thoroughly convincing.'

I was no longer listening to him. Raising a hand to my brow, I muttered: ''Mastery over death' . . . John, that is it!' I rushed to the chaise and picked up Devlin Cardew's book, looked in the index under 'mastery over death', then frantically turned to the page indicated. As I read, I felt the hot white heat of truth wash over me. 'John! We must call Inspector Stradlee at once!'

'Stradlee? Amelia, I have told you — '

'Yes, yes, and I don't care! We must convince him to listen, whatever it takes! Harry's life might be at stake!'

Sighing, John reached for the telephone, a wretched modern device that I normally detest, but which, on occasion, had its uses. While he was signalling to the exchange for a connection with Scotland Yard, a plan was forming in my head. It would take even more explaining, if not outright pleading, but it might be the only way to get the killer to drop his guard.

The upshot of the telephone call was that within the hour, both Inspectors Stradlee and Laurie were in our flat, listening as I laid out my suspicions and my plan.

'Out of the question,' Stradlee said in regards to the plan. 'It's too dangerous.'

'Mrs. Watson's instincts have produced results for us before, George,' Inspector Laurie said. 'I think we should do what she asks.'

The ferrety inspector strode around the day room, thinking, then stopped. 'All right, but since I'm the one here who will be putting my neck on the block by allowing this, I have to protect myself. So I'll do it on three conditions. One: if your theory turns out to be right, Mrs. Watson, I get the credit for it.'

'Of course,' I said.

He turned to Inspector Laurie. 'Two: since you're the one who talked me into this, Robbie, if it blows up in our faces, you're the one who's going to take the blame in front of the super.'

After a moment's thought, Inspector Laurie said, 'Agreed.'

'Three,' Inspector Stradlee went on, turning now to John, 'you're going to stop writing about a certain Yard inspector in your stories.'

'Oh, really, Stradlee — '

'Those are my terms. If I agree to this plan, you banish Inspector Lestrade from your writing forever.'

'Inspector Lestrade?' I said, recognising the name. A moment later, I realised that *Lestrade* was an anagram of *Stradlee*. At least that mystery was solved.

'Oh, very well,' John muttered. 'Inspector Lestrade is dead.'

'All right, then,' said Inspector Stradlee. 'Mind you, I'm doing this against my better judgment. Now then, Bliss doesn't know what we're up to, so I don't think he's going to make a run for it. Mrs. Watson, we'll make the telephone call you want to Bliss tonight, and then be ready by tomorrow night. I just hope you're right.'

So did I.

It seemed like an eternity before the following evening arrived. At least I had the satisfaction of learning from Inspector Laurie — whom I had persuaded to allow John and I to be present for the arrest of the killer — that the first part of the plan had been successful. 'When Bliss got that telephone call last night, his reaction was everything we'd hoped it would be,' Inspector Laurie said in the cab on the way to Fleet Street. 'He promised to pass on the message. The next call is scheduled for nine o'clock tonight.'

It was half-past eight when John and I took our places in the shadows across the street from the offices of Bliss and Co. I had convinced Inspector Laurie to let John and I be there to watch. I could see Inspector Stradlee and a couple of his men milling about, trying to appear inconspicuous, and for the most part succeeding. When the bell of a nearby church tolled nine, I held my breath.

It only took a minute. A sharp cry was heard coming inside the offices of Bliss and Co., and then a series of shouts. Then the door burst open, and a man ran out into the street, closely followed by William Bliss. From the photographs in the book, I immediately recognised the first man as Devlin Cardew — very much alive. A whistle was heard and uniformed officers suddenly appeared out of every shadow, encircling both men and detaining them. I could hear Mr. Cardew babbling: 'It was him! Gillingwater! I recognised his voice! He spoke to me from . . . from the dead! Dear God, he *came back*!' As the constables attempted to calm him, I ran past them and into the office, where Inspector Stradlee was holding a telephone receiver. Taking it from him, I said into it: 'Harry, Harry you did it!'

'So I heard, ducks,' Harry's voice responded. 'I only had the chance to give ol' Cardew a half-dozen words in Gillingwater's voice when he started screamin'.''

Inspector Stradlee took back the

receiver and barked into the telephone: 'Good work, Benbow. Now, put Sergeant Macgill on . . . Macgill? Release him. I've got the real killer.' Replacing the receiver, he turned to me with something approaching a smile. 'I owe you a debt, Mrs. Watson,' he said.

'I may ask that you repay it sometime,' I said.

The next evening's *Times* returned the story of Gillingwater's murder to the front page, only now it had the even more sensational resolution to back it up, courtesy of Bliss's confession. Apparently a series of bad investments had left Devlin Cardew not only bankrupt, but dangerously in debt, a situation that Cardew was anxious to keep quiet. James Gillingwater, however, learned of Cardew's problem, and was threatening to spread the word of his adversary's financial downfall. So with the help of his beleaguered business manager, Cardew concocted the wager — only the true stake of the bet was not a thousand pounds, as Harry had been informed, but rather Gillingwater's silence. In reality, though, Cardew was already planning to kill his enemy, removing any possibility that the spiritualist would cause trouble for him in the future.

It was quite a well-thought-through plan. In front of the house in Camden Town, Cardew had suggested a gentlemanly toast to the success of the venture, but neither Harry nor Gillingwater realised the brandy he produced was laced with a sleeping draught. After Harry fell asleep, Cardew carried the similarly slumbering Gillingwater inside, stabbed him, and smeared some of the blood on himself to make it look like he had been stabbed as well. Then he planted the empty bottle on Harry, set the bloody knife on the floor, and took his place beside Gillingwater, employing the relaxation trick he had learned in Tibet, which he later employed in his magic act, to slow down his pulse and respiration. When the police came the next day, he appeared to be dead and continued to appear to be dead until he was lodged at the morgue, at which time he simply revived himself, got up and walked out!

Bliss then hid him out in his office until Cardew could safely escape the city, and his debts.

Cardew had only miscalculated through his selection of Harry as the one to incriminate for the murders. According to Bliss's statement, having experienced Harry speaking in any number of voices, making faces, and even doing an odd dance step or two during his interview, Cardew had assumed that he was some kind of simpleton instead of a natural entertainer.

It was an incredible story, but my reading of it was interrupted by John's muttering of what sounded like 'Treadles'. I looked over and saw that he was labouring over a paper, upon which he had scratched out blocks of letters.

'Is that a word game you are playing?' I asked.

'Of sorts,' he replied. 'What do you think of 'Treadles'?'

'What are treadles?'

'Not *what*, dear; *who*. My new Scotland Yard man, Inspector Treadles.'

Suddenly, I understood: *Stradlee* . . . *Lestrade* . . . *Treadles*. A sound escaped my lips.

'Did you say something, Amelia?' John asked.

'No, darling, I only sighed.'

The Adventure of the Diamond Stickpin

'By Jove!' my husband shouted upon opening the door of our home. Had it been 'Great Scott!' or 'Good Lord!' I might not have bothered, but we have been married long enough for me to know that 'By Jove!' invariably announced something truly remarkable.

I was right: standing in our doorway was a young Indian boy — not a Bombay Indian, but rather a Red Indian, complete with headband — perhaps ten or eleven years of age.

'Are you Doc Watson?' the boy inquired of my husband.

'I am *Doctor* Watson. Who might you be?'

'Henry Two-Trees. I work for the colonel.'

'The colonel?'

'Colonel Cody, with the Wild West Show.'

'Amelia, he means Buffalo Bill!'

Oh, yes, Buffalo Bill. His Wild West Show had travelled to Britain at various times over the past fifteen years, and consisted of military riders from America and head-dressed Indians pretending to attack each other. While my experience with America was limited to passing through localities on the coat-tails of John, as he stopped in town after town on one of his lecture tours, plus one protracted stay in San Francisco, nothing I had witnessed was even remotely similar to the preposterous thrills promoted by this show. Still, it had proven immensely popular, even though I considered the man himself to be first cousin to that other colonial charlatan Mr. Barnum.

'This is extraordinary!' John declared. 'The Wild West Show is being staged in Windsor on Monday, and Colonel Cody has sent us two free passes! What's more, according to this young chap, he wants to see us beforehand. Today, if possible.'

'Darling, it is nearly four o'clock. Missy is already out shopping for dinner.'

'Yes, yes, quite.' Turning back to young Henry Two-Trees, John said: 'Please tell Colonel Cody that we would be delighted to make his acquaintance, but we cannot do it this evening. We would be happy to come tomorrow morning.' After obtaining details from the boy, John handed him a groat for his services and saw him out, practically cackling with excitement. *Heaven help me*, I thought.

If anything, John's enthusiasm had increased by the next morning, though I remained cool to the thought of a private meeting with the great Colonel Cody, whom I doubted was a real colonel at all, unless the Liars Society now offered commissions. We boarded the train at Waterloo Station to take us to Windsor, a short and pleasant enough trip. Upon detraining we engaged a cab to take us to the Great Park, in the shadow of Windsor Castle, where the Wild West Show was setting up. One group of men were erecting an enormous crescent-shaped seating area, the finished end of which was being covered with a skin of heavy canvas. At the far end of the arena were pens filled with horses, cows and, yes, buffalo. John's grin bisected his head as he watched a team of weathered sharpshooters practicing against a paper target. I, meanwhile, occupied myself with trying to keep the hem of my dress slightly above the ground so as not to collect every piece of the sawdust that covered the park.

From behind us, a voice said: 'You must be Dr. Watson,' and we turned to see a sturdily-built man in a broad-brimmed hat. 'My name is Dan Terrill,' he said, extending a hand. 'The colonel told me to keep a watch for you. Come this way, please.'

As we marched through the blizzard of activity, we caught sight of Henry Two-Trees, who stopped what he was doing — drawing pictures in the sawdust with a stick — long enough to stand up and salute, and call, 'Hello, 'tenant Dan.'

'Hiya, Chief Henry,' Mr. Terrill responded, saluting him back.

'He seems like a fine lad,' John commented.

'Yes sir, he is. He enjoys playing soldiers like that.'

'What exactly does he do here?' I asked.

'I guess you could say he's the show mascot. Colonel Cody took him in after his parents died.'

'Oh, dear. What happened to them?'

'I'm not really sure, madam. It happened before I joined the show. I've only been with the colonel about six months.'

Before long we came to a tent, and as Mr. Terrill opened the flap for us to enter, I passed by him closely enough to detect a scent coming from him, one that was as unmistakable as it was puzzling.

'That's odd, I thought the colonel would be here,' Mr. Terrill said. 'Wait here if you would, I'll go find him.'

The tent appeared to be the personal quarters of someone. It was sparsely furnished with cowhide-covered folding stools, a clothes rack, a well-worn dresser and a large travel trunk. Examining the gaudy buckskin coats on the clothes rack, I could only assume it was the quarters of the great man himself.

'I wonder why Colonel Cody wants to see us,' John said.

'What I wonder is why that man Mr. Terrill is wearing spirit gum,' I responded.

'Spirit gum?'

'You know, darling, theatrical glue used for false hair, such as beards and moustaches. It bears an odour that is unlike any other. Even twenty years after I last trod the boards I can still recognise it.'

'Perhaps Terrill plays a role in the show that requires makeup.'

'My thoughts exactly,' I said, with a smile.

Just then, Buffalo Bill himself entered the tent. He was not particularly tall, but had a strong, muscular build, not unlike Dan Terrill's in fact. His curled moustache and long, narrow grey beard were as luxurious as the photographs alleged, and his wavy, nearly white hair cascaded down onto his shoulders. 'Welcome!' he bellowed. 'You must be Dr. Watson, and you, ma'am, his good wife.'

'And you, sir, must be Dan Terrill!' I said, reaching and grabbing the bottom of his beard, which I tugged sharply.

The man cried out in surprise and pain and his whiskers remained steadfastly where they were.

'Great Scott!' John cried. 'Amelia, what . . . why . . . Colonel Cody, please let me apologise!'

'Oh dear,' was all I could muster, as I removed my hand to see that four or five long white hairs had indeed come off, pulled out by the roots. Dan Terrill then dashed into the tent, asking: 'I heard a shout. Is something wrong?'

'Colonel Cody,' I said, feeling the blush in my cheeks, 'please accept my apologies. I can explain.'

Had the man lashed out at me in anger for my incredible rudeness and ordered us back to London, I would not have been surprised. Instead, however, Colonel Cody began to laugh.

'Ma'am, you're the first person that's ever done that,' he said. 'Over the age of five, anyhow.' He then turned to his assistant and said, 'You go on, Dan, we're getting along fine in here,' and Mr. Terrill left the tent.

'I beg your forgiveness, Colonel Cody,' I said. 'It's just that I detected the scent of spirit gum on Mr. Terrill, and I therefore thought that he was having a joke at our expense, disguising himself as you.'

'Well, you're right about Dan having glue on his face,' he said, gingerly patting his beard. 'See, he stands in for me in rehearsals so I can direct the show. There's a lot of men on horseback out there, all riding like the wind, so I ask him to put on a wig and whiskers that match mine just so I can keep track of him. Sit down, please.' He motioned us to the stools, which were wobbly and not very comfortable, but I was hardly in a position to complain. 'The reason I asked you to come here, Dr. Watson, is because I have a problem,' Colonel Cody said. 'While I'm here I'm scheduled to meet with King Edward, who's actually an old friend. I was planning to wear something he gave me a few years back: a gold stickpin, encrusted with about fifty diamonds, and with the King's insignia on the head.'

'Good heavens, it must be worth a fortune,' John said.

'As far as I'm concerned it's priceless, because it's a gift of friendship between our two countries. Now, I don't want to get on my high horse about this, but when I come over here I'm considered something of an ambassador of the United States. If I went to see Bertie . . . that is, King Edward . . . without that pin, why, it would be a slap in his face.'

'So I take it the pin is missing?'

'Not just missing, Doctor, it was stolen right out of this tent. The whole place was ransacked, which made me plenty nervous, because I also had the company cashbox in here at the time, all eleven thousand pounds sterling of it.'

'Eleven thousand pounds!'

'This show has a lot of expenses, Doctor. Our animals don't stop eating just because they're on tour, and neither do our people. Since my business partner didn't come along with us on this trip, it's up to me to take care of the finances.'

'But wasn't that a huge risk, leaving that sort of sum lying around in your tent?' I asked.

'It was, and as a rule, I don't leave it here. See, this is just a dressing room. I have a suite at the Windsor Hotel, too, and I was planning to put the box in the hotel safe as soon as I was able. When I saw what happened here, you can bet I got that cashbox over to the hotel pronto, so it's safe now. My guess is whoever it was came in here looking for the cashbox but settled for the pin, not knowing the kind of situation this was going to put me in.'

'Have you called the police?' John inquired.

Colonel Cody shook his head. 'Once you get the police involved, bad press is sure to follow. I take pride that the Wild West Show has never had an ounce of bad publicity, particularly in its European tours. My first thought, frankly, was to call in your friend Sherlock Holmes, but I learned he's retired.'

As far as the public was concerned, Mr.

Holmes was retired, though I knew that was merely a charade to cover his secret activities.

'It was Dan who thought that you would be a good substitute for Holmes, Doctor, since you've been on so many cases with him. He's read all your stories, by the way.'

'I am honoured and flattered,' John said, puffing up a bit. 'Do you have any information or clues that might point to a particular person?'

'The only concrete information is that Dan caught a flash of someone rushing out of the tent right about the time the pin disappeared. He thought the fellow was wearing an Indian jacket.'

'So the thief must be an Indian.'

'I wouldn't bet on it. I've never known one of our native people to steal anything. Their culture isn't founded upon the idea of possessions like ours are.'

'So it could have been a white man dressed like an Indian in the hopes of pointing the guilt to someone else?' I offered.

'That's what I'm thinking.'

'Is there any one person you suspect?' John asked.

Colonel Cody sighed heavily. 'I hate to accuse anyone without evidence, but there's one fellow I've been keeping my eye on. He's called Utah Jim. Former military man. Used to be a crack shot and a mighty fine rider, but some years back he took a fall from his horse and broke his hip. He can't ride anymore, but I keep him on as a labourer. Unfortunately, he's developed the gambling bug. He used to come to me for advances on his salary, always with some hard-luck story or another, and then I found out it was all going down the hole at the poker table. Last time he came to me for money, I refused him, and he didn't take too kindly to that. Called me every name in the book, in fact.'

'Perhaps you should have dismissed him then and there.'

'Well,' the showman drawled, 'he was injured in my service and I kind of feel responsible for that. If it turns out it was Utah, I don't want to see him prosecuted,

I just want the pin back. Think you can help me?'

'We can certainly try,' John said.

The colonel cast another glance at me. 'We?'

'My wife has frequently aided the police with investigations.'

'No kidding!' the showman said. 'Why, that's great! I always admired women who could do a man's job. Just like Annie Oakley. She retired a couple years ago, and I wish she hadn't. She could outshoot any man I ever saw!'

I confess that my opinion of Colonel Cody was beginning to brighten.

'Now then,' he went on, 'I'm supposed to meet with the King tomorrow morning, and then we've got an early-afternoon parade past the castle, and then the show, so time's running out. I've made arrangements for you to stay over at the Windsor Hotel too, Doctor, if you need to, though I wasn't expecting two. I hope the room's big enough.'

'I'm certain it will be fine,' John said.

'And you have my complete authority to talk to anyone in the show.'

'Won't we be a bit conspicuous?' I asked.

'I've thought about that. I think the best thing is to tell people is that you're journalists too, and you're here to write an article about the show, and you need to talk to them about it.'

'Ah!' John said, reaching into his coat pocket and withdrawing a notepad. 'Now I look the part!'

'Pshaw howdy!' Colonel Cody enthused, which I took to be American for . . . well, for something.

We spent the next two hours simply wandering around the show grounds, and I abandoned any hopes of keeping my dress free of sawdust. None of the many Indians we encountered wore a beaded jacket of the type described by Dan Terrill. After stopping for a very odd lunch of something containing beans and spices in the adequately-named mess tent, we set out to resume our search. Before long, however, the run-through of the show had begun and most of the workers were focused on the rehearsal. Among the few who appeared to be at liberty was young Henry Two-Trees.

'Did you see the colonel?' the boy asked upon spotting us.

'Indeed we did,' John replied, 'and I was wondering if you might be able to tell us where a man named Utah Jim is. Is he in the rehearsal?'

'No, he is not part of the show anymore. He might be in the drink tent. It's down that way.'

The 'drink tent' turned out to be a place where the workers could stand in the shade for a bit and get a cup of cool water — and only water. Three roust-abouts were waiting under the canopy, but none of them, it turned out, was Utah Jim. 'I ain't seen him since last night,' said one of them, and the other two agreed. We took our leave and continued to stroll the grounds.

'You know, John, if this Utah person has disappeared, it does rather suggest that he — ' I stopped suddenly, having noticed something near the stable area.

'What is it, Amelia?'

'Look over there, darling. Either I have spent too much time in the sun, or that heap of sawdust has sprouted a leg.'

Rushing to the five-foot pile of woodchips that sat next to the horse pen, John began clearing away some of the sawdust, and even from a distance I could see there was someone buried there.

John called to a man by the pens: 'You there, fetch Colonel Cody at once! Tell him it is an emergency.' Catching a glimpse of the body, the man muttered something I was not able to make out, and strode off towards the arena.

'Is he dead?' I asked.

'Yes, for at least a couple of hours,' John said. 'He's been shot through the chest.'

'How dreadful!'

A minute later, we heard the heavy footsteps of Colonel Cody running up behind us. 'What is it?' he said, his white locks bouncing off his shoulders.

'Someone has made a rather clumsy attempt to hide a dead body in this sawdust heap,' John said.

'Dead body!' Colonel Cody stepped up to the body and took off his hat. 'That is Utah Jim,' he pronounced. Now I stepped forward just enough to see as much of the burly figure as I wished to. Colonel Cody knelt down and began examining the body for himself. 'Forgive what must seem like insensitivity, Doctor, but I have to check his pockets,' he said. After thoroughly searching the man's clothes, he shook his head and stood up. 'No pin.'

'Something else is conspicuously missing,' John pronounced. 'A gunshot wound like that should have produced a good deal of blood, but there is hardly a trace of it in the sawdust.'

'Meaning?'

'Possibly that the man was killed elsewhere and his body was moved here.'

'Something bad is going on, I can smell it,' Colonel Cody declared, and I had to agree with him, even though all I could actually smell were the animal pens.

'I'm sorry, Colonel, but the police must be contacted now,' John said.

The showman nodded his shaggy head. 'I'm afraid you're right, Doctor. But do this much for me: don't present yourselves to the police. Let me say that I found the body.'

'To what end?' I asked.

'So you can keep looking for the pin. Is it a deal?'

'Very well,' John replied.

'Now I'd better go and call off the run-through until after I've dealt with the police. Be careful, now.'

Once he had gone, I asked: 'Is it wise to deceive the police like that?'

'Likely not,' John sighed, 'but if we were to step forward we would have to tell the police what we were doing here, and suddenly a crime of passion would escalate into the very international controversy that Colonel Cody is striving to avoid. The best course is to do as he asks and remain quiet, at least for a little while longer.'

'Do you really think we will find the pin now?'

'I cannot say. But assuming that Utah Jim stole it to pay off his debts — an assumption we must make at this point — it seems logical that whoever killed him also relieved him of the pin.'

'Which would exonerate the man to whom Jim was indebted, don't you think?' I said. 'I mean, Jim was going to give him the pin anyway, so why would he have to kill for it?'

'But what if he was *not* going to give him the pin?' John countered. 'What if Utah Jim decided to keep it; or what if he were suddenly overwhelmed with guilt, and decided to return it to his employer? If that were the case, the only way his creditor could get it would be to kill him and take it. In any event, I believe we should try to identify the man to whom Utah Jim was in debt.'

We accosted as many people as we could, using our cover as visiting journalists. John's lines of questioning invariably ran to each person's leisure activities, hoping that one would mention card playing. After interviewing (by my count) thirty-seven cowboys and nineteen Indians — only a fraction of the show's total cast — our task began to appear as futile as it was tiring. But then we came upon one particular cowboy named with the improbable name of Hondo Sharpe, who informed us that Utah Jim had repeatedly been the victim of one Zeb

Parker at the gaming tables. Encouraged by this news, we set out to find Mr. Parker. Unfortunately, it appeared that he, too, had disappeared from the Wild West Show.

After another dozen or so interviews, our spirits, not to mention our energy, began to ebb. Darkness was encroaching and we were no closer to finding the stickpin than we had been at the day's start. 'I've not a clue as to what to do next,' John sighed, dismally.

'My suggestion,' I replied, 'is to take up the kind offer of the hotel room, as I am weary, hungry, and have an army of little sawdust slivers crawling up my legs. Perhaps something will come to us there.' Finding a cab, we rode to the hotel in silence.

The room, as Colonel Cody had predicted, was small, but adequate, and while we had not come prepared for an overnight stay, it was a relief simply to sit in a comfortable chair and freshen up at the basin. 'Maybe we are looking at this the wrong way, darling,' I said. 'Perhaps the pin was not stolen for its monetary value, but taken deliberately.'

'But for what reason?' John asked.

'To embarrass Colonel Cody in his meeting with the King? We may be dealing with an angry, disgruntled employee of the show, not an impoverished one.'

'Then what about the death of Utah Jim?'

'Perhaps it is completely unrelated to the theft, and simply the result of his gambling debts.'

'And that the other fellow, Parker, fled the show after killing him . . . it's possible, I suppose. But that still gets us nowhere regarding the diamond stickpin.'

'Look, John, you and I both know His Majesty, too,' I said, relating the unlikely truth that, through Sherlock Holmes's brother Mycroft, an advisor to the Crown, we had become acquaintances of the King. 'Why don't we simply present ourselves to him and explain why Colonel Cody is not wearing the pin? Surely he would understand.'

John sighed. 'You may be right, Amelia. It just galls me to admit that we have failed. The colonel put his trust in us and we have let him down.'

'There is still time for a clue to reveal itself,' I said, though inwardly I strongly doubted it. 'Until then, however, we really must speak with Colonel Cody.'

We stopped at the hotel desk to see if Colonel Cody had returned for the evening and were told he had not. 'He still must be at the arena,' I sighed, not wanting at all to go back there, particularly in the darkness of night. But, having no other options, we hailed a cab and went back to the Windsor Great Park.

Electric lamps had been set up on poles throughout the grounds so that there was enough light to see. There was little visible activity going on, though we could hear music coming from somewhere. We proceeded to Colonel Cody's dressing tent, only to find him with another man, a rugged specimen that we had not before encountered.

'Oh, I am sorry to interrupt you, Colonel Cody,' John said. 'We need to speak with you, but we can come back when you are free.'

'No, no, Doctor, I'm glad you're here,' the showman said. 'Maybe you can make head or tail out of what Zeb here is saying.'

'Zeb Parker?' I asked, and the man nodded. John and I exchanged an excited glance.

'These folks are here to help, Zeb, so tell 'em what you told me.'

'I . . . I shot Utah Jim,' the man said, miserably, 'but I did it out of mercy. I found him behind the main tent, and he was . . . I don't know . . . he was actin' like a mad dog or somethin'. His face was blue and he was lyin' on the ground, twitchin'.'

'His face was blue, you say?' John asked.

'Yeah, like he was chokin' or somethin'. And he tried to talk, but it was like his face was frozen. All I could hear was something that sounded like 'the loot'.'

'The lute, like a harp?' I asked, thinking of the music I had just heard.

'More likely 'l-o-o-t', as in stolen money,' Colonel Cody said.

Zeb Parker went on: 'I didn't like Utah

much, but I near couldn't stand seein' him go through whatever he was goin' through, so I went to my tent, got my six-shooter, and . . . put him out of his misery. Then I hid him in the sawdust pile.'

'Did you tell this to the police?'

Zeb Parker shook his head. 'I knew the police wouldn't believe me. They'd think I just shot him in cold blood.'

'Blood . . . ' John uttered, as though something had struck him. 'Mr. Parker, when you shot him, did the wound bleed?'

Zeb Parker knit his brows in thought. 'Now that you mention it, no, hardly any at all.'

'Then I can assure you that you did not kill Utah Jim.'

'But I — '

'Oh, you may have shot him but you did not kill him. He was already dead. He had been poisoned.'

'Poisoned?' Colonel Cody gasped.

'Curare, if I'm not mistaken. It is a rapid-acting poison derived from certain plants in South America that causes the very symptoms you describe, including the bluish pallor and the muscle paralysis. The pallor subsides after an hour or so, which is why he was no longer blue when we found him. But the fact that your gunshot wound drew no blood indicates that he was already dead, for cadavers do not bleed.'

'Damn!' Zeb Parker declared.

'I will make a report to the local police before we leave Windsor saying exactly that, so you have nothing to fear,' John said, and a relieved-looking Zeb Parker was dismissed and left the tent to go back to his duties. Colonel Cody, however, looked ashen.

'I know this must be upsetting,' John told him.

'More than you think, Doctor,' the showman replied. 'I've heard of curare before. I've heard tell of Indians tipping arrowheads into it so that it instantly killed their enemies.'

'Heavens,' I uttered. 'Taken with Mr. Terrill's testimony of a beaded jacket, it does appear that we have narrowed down the suspect list to Indians.'

Before we could say any more, a single gunshot came from outside the tent. Colonel Cody looked alarmed. 'I forbid shooting after dark!' he barked, practically leaping through the tent flaps. John and I followed, only to find a group of people beginning to circle around something on the ground. Rushing towards it, we soon saw that the mysterious goings-on of the Wild West Show had claimed another victim: Zeb Parker lay sprawled in the sawdust.

'Dear God,' I muttered, as John quickly examined him and pronounced him dead, this time definitely from a gunshot wound.

Colonel Cody looked stunned. 'I'm sorry I dragged the two of you into this,' he said grimly. 'The situation has got far beyond stolen jewellery, and I think it would be safer for the both of you to go back to the hotel and stay there. And as soon as I can find Henry, I'll send him there as well. He doesn't need to be around all this.'

We took him at his word and returned immediately, repairing to the hotel café to talk. 'Should we tell the police to check the water in the water tent for poison?' I asked.

'No,' John replied. 'Colonel Cody reminded me of something when he spoke of Indians using the poison on their arrowheads. Curare must be administered subcutaneously in order to work. Taken orally it has no effect.'

While we were talking, Henry Two-Trees appeared in the café, much to the consternation of the waiter. I looked his way and then froze. 'Good heavens, John, look at what he has on!'

The young Indian wore an intricately beaded jacket!

John flagged him over and bade him sit at the table, which he did. 'The colonel is talking to all the men,' he reported. 'He might have to call off the show tomorrow.'

'That jacket you're wearing is quite interesting, Henry,' I said, changing the subject. 'Have you had it long?'

'My mother made it for me,' he replied, quietly.

'Does Mr. Terrill know you have a jacket like this?'

''Tenant Dan? I don't know.'

John smiled at the boy. 'I'm sure that if Lieutenant Dan did know, he would have said so.'

Henry frowned. 'Why do you call him '*leff-tenant*'? He's a *loo*-tenant.'

'Well, Henry, that's one of the differences of speech between American English and British English. The word is spelled the same, but here we pronounce it *leff*. *Loo*, I'm afraid, means something entirely different in England.'

That was when the lightning bolt struck me. And not only me, I saw, but John as well. I raised my hand to my forehead while he simply stood up at the table. 'I think I know who did it!' I shouted.

'I think I know how!' John added.

Little Henry looked quite startled as we turned on him. 'Henry, were you to stay in Colonel Cody's room tonight?'

'Yes.'

'No, you mustn't,' I said. 'It might not be safe. You had better stay with us.'

'My dear, our room is barely big enough for two,' John pointed out.

186

'Henry, you're not afraid to stay in a room by yourself?'

'Of course not.'

'That's the lad. We'll get a separate room for you. I will see the manager about it at once.' John dashed out of the café, and in short order was able to get the boy his own room, only a few doors down from ours. We made sure he was locked in for his own safety. It was already after ten o'clock, but there were still preparations that had to be made to trap a killer, most of which John handled from the front desk of the hotel. Afterwards, there was little to do but wait until morning.

Sleeping was not easy, but I forced myself into at least a couple hours of slumber. John stayed up the entire night, fuelled by that charge of excitement that overtakes him whenever he is on a case.

Sleep or no, by eight the next morning we were in the hotel lobby, waiting.

It was nearly an hour later when Buffalo Bill Cody descended the stairs into the lobby. 'Good morning, Colonel Cody, I hope you slept well,' the hotel manager bade him, as per our instructions.

'Quite,' the showman uttered, continuing to walk towards the door. Right before he got there, John and I stepped in front of him.

'Colonel Cody,' John began, 'I see that you found your pin.' As we suspected, the diamond stickpin — whose head, bearing a carved 'E', a Roman numeral seven, and a small crown, for Edward XVII, was even more stunning than I had imagined — was set firmly in Buffalo Bill's lapel.

'Hmmm, oh, yes,' he said, gruffly. 'Now I have to be on my way.'

'Not so fast, sir,' said Inspector Steele of the local constabulary, who had materialised from behind the desk, along with a half-dozen other officers. Upon seeing them, Buffalo Bill turned and delivered a look of pure hatred towards us, then reached for the pin.

'Watch out for his hand!' John shouted, and instantly, the constables were upon him, pulling back his arms and forcing him to drop the pin on the floor. 'Nobody touch it!' the inspector commanded.

Buffalo Bill fought, but he was easily outnumbered, and within seconds the policemen had him subdued.

'Allow me,' I said, stepping towards the struggling man. Grasping his beard, I gave it a sharp tug, and this time it came off in my hand. Similarly taking the edge of his moustache, I removed it as well, then pulled off his hat and the long, flowing white wig, revealing Colonel Cody's rehearsal stand-in, Lieutenant Dan Terrill.

Meanwhile, the police inspector was on the floor, carefully picking up the diamond stickpin with a handkerchief. 'So this is where the poison is, eh?'

'Yes,' John confirmed. 'Terrill planned all along to replace Colonel Cody for his meeting with His Majesty. That, in fact, was why he joined the show in the first place, so he could get close enough to the King. He stole the stickpin to use it as a weapon, dipped it in curare, and then planned to wear it into his audience with His Majesty. At the first opportunity he would then stab him with it, thereby assassinating him!'

A chorus of gasps rose from the constables, who tightened their grips on Dan Terrill to the point where they forced the powerful villain to his knees.

From behind us, the real Buffalo Bill Cody emerged, his arm around a very sad-looking Henry Two-Trees. ''Tenant Dan lied,' the boy said, miserably.

'I didn't want to believe it either,' Colonel Cody said, shaking his head. 'So you think he killed both Utah Jim and Zeb?'

John nodded. 'Zeb Parker was killed to keep him from talking to the police. But the attack on Utah Jim was to test the poison before he used it on His Majesty. Jim possessed roughly the same build as the King, so Terrill was able to gauge how quickly the poison would act on a man of that size. Longer than he expected, as it turned out, since Jim lived long enough to get away and attract the attention of Zeb Parker.'

'And utter his last words, 'the loot',' I said. 'At first we accepted the theory that it signified money, but a conversation with Henry made us realise that what

Utah Jim was actually trying to say was *the lieutenant*, naturally using the American pronunciation of the world. He was identifying his killer.'

'The rest you know, Colonel,' John went on. 'Not realising that anyone had guessed his plan, Terrill followed through with his abduction of you, drugging you and putting you out of commission long enough for the substitution to take place.'

I knew that the police, having been alerted by John to the plan last night, had found Colonel Cody tied up and secreted inside the large trunk in his tent. By then Mr. Terrill had returned to the hotel in disguise. 'We surmise,' I rejoined, 'that after stabbing the King he would get away in all the confusion, doff his disguise and disappear, leaving you, Colonel, to try and defend yourself. The only thing we cannot guess is why he was so bent on assassinating His Majesty King Edward.'

All eyes were now on Dan Terrill. 'Why?' he sneered, pronouncing it *vie*. 'Because certain influential men from my homeland were willing to pay me a Kaiser's ransom to do so, that is why.' The man's American accent had completely disappeared and was replaced by a German one. 'Some of us consider the European treaties of 'Edward the Peace-maker' to be a veiled threat to the motherland. The final provocation was the Entente Cordiale with France. The time to take action had come.'

'Sweet Jesus, you're a spy!' Colonel Cody said in disbelief. 'This was going on all this time; and yet it was you, Dan, who encouraged me to get Dr. Watson to investigate the theft. If you hadn't done that, you probably would have got away with this.'

The man who called himself Dan Terrill spat out a bitter laugh. '*Ja!* I suggested this Watson because I had read enough of his stories to know that he is a barely-functioning idiot! He never solves a case, it is always Holmes! I knew you would call someone in, so I figured: why not a bungling fool? I never expected anything from him but total confusion. I even gave him misleading information, like that stupid beaded jacket. Yet he solved it! *Mein Gott*, the first case he ever solves has to be my own! What a joke!'

'Please allow me the satisfaction of pointing out your stupid mistake,' I said. 'You failed to take into account my husband's skills as a writer. Sherlock Holmes's Dr. Watson may be a dull-witted fellow, but he is a literary creation. The real John H. Watson is shrewd and intelligent. You failed because you over-estimated one and underestimated the other.'

Once the constables had taken the still-struggling Mr. Terrill outside, Inspector Steele said: 'I'll have to take this pin down for analysis.'

'Would it be possible for me to get it back by, say, ten o'clock?' Colonel Cody asked. 'I kind of have to wear it to an appointment.'

'I understand, sir, and it will be back in time,' he said, and then marched briskly out of the hotel.

I could see a solitary tear running down the face of Henry Two-Trees, and my heart went out to the boy. Colonel Cody saw it too, and knelt down to him. 'I know how much you liked Lieutenant

Dan, son,' he said. 'I did too. You go on back to my room and we'll talk about it when I get there.' Without a word, Henry Two-Trees turned and walked, soldier-like, up the stairs.

Colonel Cody sighed heavily as he turned to us. 'Thanking you seems insufficient. So do free passes to the show. What else can I do for you two?'

'Well, may I have your permission to write this story up someday?' John asked.

'By all means,' the showman grinned. 'I'll be real curious to see how it comes out, since according to your missus here, you're a bigger prevaricator than even old Ned Buntline.'

John actually turned red. 'My stories are not *that* far removed from the truth.'

'Now, darling,' I said, 'you are far too modest.'

The Adventure of the
Headless Beggar

It was not like John to be so late. I
glanced once more at the clock, paced
back across the room and looked out
through the window into the dark night. I
knew he was not with his regular patients
for the simple fact that he no longer had
regular patients. Of late, his devotion both
to his writing and the lecture circuit had
occupied so much of his time that his
medical practice had dwindled to practically nothing. He had not spoken of
meetings today with his tour agents or his
publishers, so where on earth was he?

I had a dreadful thought: what if
Sherlock Holmes had once again suddenly rematerialised in London and had
conscripted him for yet another middle-
aged *Boy's Own* adventure? The very
thought of my otherwise rational husband

being drawn back into a life of hiding in bushes, brandishing pistols, or racing like a demon to catch the next train to heaven-knew-where in order to combat heaven-knew-what made me shudder. But, when last heard from, Mr. Holmes had been sent on some sort of mission by his brother Mycroft, its duration being as great a secret as its nature. As far as I knew, the great detective might presently be enjoying a whiskey and soda in a club in Pall Mall, or he might be in a tent in Timbuktu.

I continued to fret about it until the front door opened some twenty minutes later and familiar footsteps announced his presence at last.

'Hello, Amelia,' John said as he entered the room. Before I could say a word of recrimination over his lateness, he glanced around and remarked: 'I see you have nearly been driven to distraction with worry. I am sorry about that.'

'How can you tell I have been driven to distraction?'

'Simplicity itself. When I left this

morning, I observed a stack of magazines here,' he said, pointing to a small, round table that we keep next to the wing chair. 'Now I observe they are over there.' He redirected his finger to the chaise longue by the window. 'Clearly, my absence has made you nervous, and to try and calm yourself you picked up a magazine, but found yourself too agitated to read it. So you paced to the chaise and laid it down, then came back and absentmindedly picked up another, repeating the process until the entire stack of magazines ended up, unread, on the chaise. There can be no other explanation for the magazines moving across the room.' Satisfied, he hung up his hat and put his walking stick in the elephant's foot umbrella stand.

At that moment our young maid Missy bustled in, curtseyed politely to John, and then noticed the littered chaise. 'Oh, I'm sorry, mum,' she said, rushing over and gathering up the magazines. 'I forgot to put these back on the table after dusting.' She returned them to their proper place, and bustled back out.

John turned quite red, and while I tried

not to laugh, I could not quite prevent it. 'Actually, darling, you were right,' I said, massaging his brow and ego at the same time, 'I was becoming anxious.'

'I was called in unexpectedly for a consultation.'

'With Dr. Fennyman?'

'No, with Inspector Laurie.'

'What does Scotland Yard want of you now?'

John regarded me with a grave expression. 'Another one has been found, Amelia.'

There was no need for him to elaborate. I knew immediately what he meant. For nearly a fortnight it had been the only story in the headlines, the only subject spoken of in London's businesses, restaurants, theatres, and other gathering places: the deranged killer who had been preying upon the beggars and vagrants of London, decapitating them and leaving their headless bodies on the grounds of several churches in the city's East End. So far there had been three victims of 'the Chopper', as the press had dubbed him, and not since the tragic case some months ago of a small boy who had accidentally been shot and killed by a constable firing at a fleeing criminal had there been such a public display of outrage directed towards the Metropolitan Police.

'This one was found at St. Botolph's without Aldgate,' John went on. 'Laurie called me in because of a singular circumstance regarding the body.'

'What was that?'

'The head was still with it.'

'Then it was not the work of the Chopper?'

'Oh, indeed it was. The head was still there but it was not attached. Laurie wanted me to tell him whether the head and body belonged together, and judging from the matching subcutaneous cut marks on both halves of the neck, they did. He also wanted to know if I agreed that the man had been killed somewhere else and moved near the church, and I did, given the general lack of blood at the site. But mostly, he wanted to know if there was an evidence that the perpetrator was skilled in the cutting of flesh, such as might indicate a surgeon, or perhaps a soldier, or even a professional meat butcher; but the signs of hacking were too great for that to be the case.'

'*Please*, darling,' I said, placing a hand over my stomach.

'Oh, I am sorry. Sometimes I forget not everyone is as accustomed to viewing the human body in distress with the objectivity of a physician. Still, I cannot get the image of that poor devil out of my mind.'

Missy then reappeared to ask: 'Do you want me to start supper now?'

'Yes,' I replied, 'and given the hour, I had best help you if we want to dine before midnight.'

'I have a better idea, Amelia,' John said. 'What do you say to a late supper at Simpson's on the Strand to make up for my tardiness? Missy, you may have the night off. Take in a show at the music hall if you like.'

The girl's eyes widened with alarm. 'If you don't mind, sir, I'll stay right here. I don't want to set foot outside with that maniac on the loose!' The press had certainly done its job of spreading terror throughout the city well.

By the time John and I got to Simpson's we had passed so many eager news vendors shouting out teasing details of the latest murder that it was hard to think of anything else, which was not terribly conducive to formulating a good appetite. After a rather solemn supper, we returned to Queen Anne Street and our now equally solemn home.

For the next two days I actively strove to put all thought of the horrendous crimes out of my head. It all came flooding back, however, on Thursday evening when I happened to look over at John, who was seated behind his desk intently working with a pencil on a piece of paper. 'What are you doing, darling?' I asked.

'Hmm?' he uttered, looking up. 'Oh, nothing, really. Sketching.'

'Sketching?' Peering over his shoulder I saw a very professional drawing of the head of a man who was virtually hairless, and had a long lifetime's worth of trouble etched into his face. 'John, that is excellent! All this time I had no idea you were an artist.'

'*Artist* is too strong a word, I think,' he rejoined, 'although I used to do a lot of sketching as a youth.'

'Why did you stop?'

'Oh, there was little time for it in Baker Street, and it tended to annoy Holmes anyway.'

'Yes, I am sure the discovery that you could do something better than he was a nettle in his side.'

'I would hardly say that.'

No, of course not. John would hardly say anything that cast a shadow over the character of the Great Detective, no matter how true it was, but I decided not to press it. Glancing again at the drawing, I said: 'That man has such misery in his face. Who is it?'

'The poor beggar who was the latest victim of the Chopper.'

I left him to his sketching. Within the half-hour our doorbell sounded, and Missy welcomed in Inspector Laurie of Scotland Yard. 'I am afraid I am here officially,' the inspector said grimly, doffing his bowler hat as he came into the day room. 'Dr. Watson, I require your help again. There has been yet another one, this time outside of St. Martin Orgar in Cannon Street. This one's head is missing, like the first three.'

'Good Lord. Have you at least been able to find a connection between the victims?' John asked. 'Other than their being found in front of churches, I mean?'

The inspector shook his head. 'We cannot even identify most of them, even the one whose head was left. We thought we had a lead on the first one because of a tattoo on his chest, or what we thought was a tattoo. It turned out to be ink, for some reason painted on in concentric circles, like an archer's target.'

'Why on earth would someone do that?' I asked.

'I wish I knew, Mrs. Watson. The poor blighter tonight had money in his pocket, which says to me that he was killed before he had a chance to get to a tavern, though none of the local publicans or gin shop owners could recognise the clothes on the body. The rest of the victims either had empty pockets or were carrying the kinds of scraps you can pick from the streets, like old bits of tiles and orange peels. This entire matter is a mess, and now the government has joined the news hawks in sounding the hue and cry against us. Sir Melville himself came under attack in Parliament today for failing to capture the killer.'

Sir Melville Macnaghten was the head of the Yard's Criminal Investigation Department.

'Can you not put men around every church in the East End?' John asked.

'I have men around them already, but I cannot reassign the entire force. Even if I could, what if the next one were to turn up in Lambeth? It is impossible to surround every church in the city.'

John sighed. 'Very well, how can I be of service this time?'

'I would like you to look at this body as well and see if you concur with the coroner's findings regarding the time of death,' he said.

John hastened away with the inspector.

He did not return until sometime after one in the morning, and by then he was in quite a state of agitation. 'It is maddening!' he cried. 'Murderers generally wish to conceal the bodies of their victims. This one flaunts them! But for what purpose?'

'It is late, darling, come to bed,' I beseeched. 'There will be plenty of time to worry about it tomorrow.'

'I suppose so,' John said. 'Though I fear that the worst part of this wretched business has not yet come to pass.'

How right he was.

No Chopper murders were reported for the next three days, effectively plunging the entire of London into a fog-like cloud of fear, awaiting the next dreadful act. Then on Monday evening our telephone rang insistently — a wretched jangling sound that I detest — and John answered it. His face blanched as he listened, then he moaned: 'Good God! How could the wretch not have been seen? I see. Yes, of course, Inspector, I will come right down.'

'Another one?' I asked, as soon as he

had replaced the receiver.

'No . . . another *three*. The fiend managed to plant three bodies on the same night — one at St. Sepulchre, one at St. Benet Gracechurch, and one at St. Dunstan in the East. At least he was seen this time, or nearly so. One of the constables stationed at St. Leonard's saw a man shoving a bundle off a dray cart, which then sped away. The bundle turned out to be another headless victim, though it was too dark to clearly see the driver, the cart or the horse.'

'I suppose you are leaving again?'

'Yes, Laurie wants me to examine the bodies again. Three more, all without heads.' He picked up his sketch of the fourth victim. 'Why was this beggar's head left with the body? It makes absolutely no sense. If only Holmes were still in the city. He would put paid to this miserable affair before another innocent victim had to die.'

Perhaps; perhaps not, I thought, knowing that Mr. Holmes had actually failed in far more cases than John was willing to reveal to his reading public, though all I said was, 'Do be careful, darling.'

'Of course I shall, my dear, though I daresay I will be late once more, so there is no need to wait up for me.'

I took him at his word and turned in shortly after eleven o'clock. I have no idea when he returned home, though he arose far later than usual the next morning and remained in a sombre mood throughout the morning.

The Illustrated London News was having a field day with their account of the triple murders and even featured a quote from John, who was identified as 'a renowned medical expert who was brought into the case by the desperate CID'.

'I don't wish to see it,' he said glumly, pushing the paper away when I offered it to him.

'Really, John, you are acting as though these murders are somehow your fault,' I chastised him.

'I am fully aware that they are not my fault.'

'Then why are you taking this so personally?'

'Because I can do nothing to solve them!' he cried, with uncharacteristic fury. 'Why can I not be of some real help to the police? Why must I always be the follower, the sounding board for someone else? Why cannot I be as clever as — ?'

'Oh, for heaven's sake, John,' I interrupted, 'I have heard all this before. Why can't you be as clever as Sherlock Holmes? Because you are not he, and honestly, I am happy that you are not!'

He gazed back at me with an injured expression. 'I was about to ask why I cannot be as clever as *you*, Amelia.'

I stood there, dumbstruck, cursing my own insensitivity.

'I am going out for a bit,' he muttered, and taking up his hat and stick, he left.

As I tried to figure out how I could possibly make it up to him, Missy appeared, polish cloth in hand, and began working on the tabletops, singing a strange, repetitive tune that ended with the grotesque line of the Chopper removing a head!

'Good heavens, child, what sort of dreadful ditty was that?' I demanded sourly.

'It's the 'Bull's Eyes and Targets' song, mum,' she replied. 'When I was a little girl, we used to play games to it. All this business of the Chopper reminded me of it, and I haven't been able to get it out of my head.'

'Try harder, for heaven's sake, and if it does happen to remain in your head, please be so good as to leave it there.'

'Yes'm, sorry, mum.' She abashedly went on with her dusting.

I went over to the chaise to lie down, but was no sooner supine than the words she had been singing struck me, and I suddenly lurched upright again. 'Missy, what did you say that song was called?'

'My own mum always called it 'Bull's Eyes and Targets' when she sang it to me, but I've heard it called 'Oranges and Lemons' too.'

'Could you sing it for me again?'

'But mum, I thought you wanted me to stop.'

'I have changed my mind. Please, Missy.'

She started anew, this time singing more loudly and clearly:

'Bull's eyes and targets, say the bells
    of St. Margaret's;
Brickbats and tiles, say the bells of
    St. Giles;
Oranges and Lemons, say the bells
    of St. Clements;
Old Father Baldpate, say the slow
    bells of Aldgate;
Halfpence and farthings, say the
    bells of St. Martin's;
When will you pay me? say the bells
    of Old Bailey;
When I grow rich, say the bells at
    Shoreditch;
Pray, when will that be? say the bells
    of Stepney;
I do not know, says the great bell at
    Bow.
Here comes a candle to light you to
    bed;
Here comes the chopper to chop off
    your head.'

The last line was delivered with a

shudder. Even so, I made her run through it again while I jotted the words down on a sheet of paper. As I stared at them, a cold sense of horror grew within me. The last half did not make much sense, but the first half of the verse did only too well. According to Inspector Laurie, the body found outside St. Margaret's had had a target painted on it — *bull's eyes and targets*; another had tiles in its pockets — *brickbats and tiles*; and another orange peels — *oranges and lemons*. The body found at St. Martin's Orgar had money, and I would be willing to wager that it was in the form of *halfpence and farthings*. Then my eye fell on John's sketch of the victim that was found outside St. Botolph's without Aldgate, and I knew why his head had been left. How long, I wondered, had the murderer looked for a victim who was of the right age and hairless enough to stand in for *Old Father Baldpate?*

I dashed to the telephone and, ignoring my hatred for the device, signalled for the exchange operator. 'Connect me immediately with Inspector Robert Laurie of

Scotland Yard,' I said. As it turned out he was not in, though a sergeant working on the case with him took my message, which was to send him to Queen Anne Street as soon as he arrived back. 'Tell him I believe I have found the connection between the Chopper killings,' I related, then rang off and returned to the chaise to think.

When John returned some time later, I laid out the evidence for him and watched his dark mood instantly give way to the kind of excitement he exhibits when involved in a case. 'The last three fit as well,' he declared. 'St. Sepulchre Holborn is a stone's throw from the Old Bailey, St. Benet Gracechurch is at Shoreditch and St. Dunstan's at Stepney. But what does it all mean?'

'It means we were dealing with a far from commonplace killer,' I replied.

Minutes later the telephone rang and John picked it up. 'Yes, Inspector,' I heard him say, 'Amelia deduced it and I believe she is on to something, but it is too complex to explain over the telephone. Can we come down to the Yard? Fine, as soon as possible.' By mid-afternoon, when those more blessed with leisure were enjoying high tea, we were sitting in Inspector Laurie's office at New Scotland Yard.

'The examination of the pockets of the last three victims revealed a bill, a sweepstakes ticket and a calendar page,' the inspector was saying, 'and here it is, all of it. The bill — 'When will you pay me?'; the ticket — 'When I grow rich'; and the calendar — 'When will that be?' It was right there in front of us the entire time. A child could have seen this, but we missed it!'

'We missed it because we are not children,' I said. 'We left the world of nursery rhymes long ago.'

'But why has the killer chosen an old children's rhyme upon which to hang his crimes?' John wondered.

'We will learn that when we catch the mongrel behind this,' Inspector Laurie said, 'and here — ' He jabbed a finger down on the word *Bow*. ' — is where we will find him. St. Mary-Le-Bow in Cheapside, the last church. We'll be there waiting, every man we can spare, and after I've taken him into custody, we'll discover his motives.' The inspector's face was flushed with triumph as he spoke. It appeared that the dreadful case was all but concluded. So why did I have a horrible little feeling that there was something terribly amiss about it?

That feeling remained even after we arrived back home, and I am afraid I spent the evening in a sullen and preoccupied manner, which, as John was quick to point out, was not like me at all. 'Are you not feeling well?' he asked, ever the physician.

'I am fine, but there is something is not right about this entire matter.'

'Are you having second thoughts about your theory regarding the Chopper?'

'Only his motives. This brute has killed eight men that we know of, has transported their bodies to exact locations, and planted clues with diabolical care on their persons, clues that deliberately point to an exact solution to the riddle. He must have known that his demented game would be detected. If I

214

had not made the connection with that nursery rhyme, surely someone else would have. It is almost as though he desperately wanted this riddle to be solved — but why? Why would he deliberately lead the police to a specific location?'

'Perhaps he wishes to be captured,' John offered. 'That is not unknown amongst criminals.'

'No, darling, I feel there is something else at play here.'

'Diversion, then. While the force descends upon Bow Church, he plans a killing elsewhere in the city.'

'Perhaps, though a diversion seems redundant for a criminal as stealthy as this one. No, there must be . . . oh, dear!' I raised my hand to my forehead as if to massage away a headache, though I felt no physical pain, only terror.

'I know that gesture,' John said. 'What have you deduced?'

'Insane as it sounds, it is the only thing that fits,' I cried. 'John, the killer is luring the police into a trap!'

'Hardly that, I should think. There will

be far too many officers to ambush.'

'Not if it is done all at once. That must be what the penultimate line means!' John looked at me with a perplexed expression. 'Listen, darling, the rhyme says, 'Here comes a candle to light you to bed'. What does that imply to you?'

'Frankly, nothing.'

'Dynamite, John! The killer wants to lure the police into Bow Church and then light them to their rest permanently, like a modern-day Guy Fawkes! He is going to blow up the church!'

'Good Lord! Who would hate the police so much as to do such a thing?'

'We can worry about that later. Now we must get to Inspector Laurie and tell him!'

'He was going straight to the church,' John said. 'I pray we are not too late!' Dashing down to the street, he hailed the first cab we saw and barked to the driver: 'Bow Church, and hurry!'

'Yer soul must need savin' orful bad, guv'ner,' the cabman muttered back, as he spurred his steed into action.

The journey to the East End seemed

agonisingly slow, though it was likely more due to my impatience than heavier-than-usual carriage traffic. Still, the light of day had all but disappeared by the time we reached Cheapside. As St. Mary-Le-Bow came into view, the police presence announced itself. In fact, a cotillion of constables stopped the cab as we neared the church.

'Hold 'er up!' one of the PCs called, and once the cab had stopped, he poked his head inside. 'Sorry, but this block is off-limits for a bit.' Then laying eyes on John, he said, 'Oh, it's Dr. Watson, isn't it?'

'Yes it is,' John said, 'and we have reason to believe that all of you are in great danger. We must speak to Inspector Laurie at once!'

'He's detained right now, sir.'

'Then interrupt him! Lives are at stake, and if they are lost, it will be on your head!'

That was argument enough for the constable, who helped us out of the cab and then escorted us through police lines until we came upon Inspector Laurie, near the front door of the church, talking with three of his subordinates. All had weapons drawn. 'Inspector Laurie!' I called.

He turned and then dashed towards us. 'What are you two doing here? Whatever it is, you must go away immediately. If our man arrives as expected, there could be trouble, and God knows the last thing the force needs is another innocent bystander shot.'

'There may be more trouble than you can imagine if you do not get every officer out of that church immediately,' John said.

'What are you talking about?'

'I believe it may be set to explode,' I told him.

'What?'

'For heaven's sake, man, you have known us long enough to realise that Amelia is not given to irrational pro-nouncements,' John cried. 'She has her reasons, and you must trust her on this.'

The inspector looked back and forth between us, and then muttered, 'All right, though if you are wrong and this fellow gets away, the next head to be severed in the city will be mine.' Turning to his men, he barked: 'Evacuate the church. Get everyone out.'

Now the officers looked confused. 'But sir — ' one began.

'*Now!*'

They dashed in immediately and ordered all of the policemen out. Moments later, a river of dark blue came flooding through the doors of the church, carrying with it a protesting elderly man with white hair and a black cassock. Once outside, he marched up to the inspector. 'Really, sir,' he said indignantly, 'why must I be forced to leave? I am, after all, the sexton of this church, and it is my responsibility — '

'It is my responsibility to keep you alive,' the inspector fired back. 'This church may be wired with explosives. Is everyone out, Sergeant Tallis?'

'Yes sir,' one of the officers crisply replied.

'Good. Prepare the men to evacuate the houses around here on my orders.'

The sexton approached the inspector

again. 'You must at least let me go back in to save the chalices,' he begged.

'I cannot risk it,' Inspector Laurie replied. 'You must get out of the immediate area. Tallis, take the sexton somewhere.'

'Where to, sir?' Sergeant Tallis asked.

'To a pub, I don't care! Just get him away from here!' Turning to us, he added: 'That goes for the two of you as well.'

We had little choice but to acquiesce, though as the sergeant walked us away, the sexton continued to protest. 'No no, stop, there still might be someone in there, one of the parishioners,' he said. 'I saw him inside earlier, but I never saw him leave.'

I stopped walking. 'Someone arrived tonight that you did not see leave?'

'Yes, yes, it was poor Mr. Canning. He has been distraught since the death of his son.'

'Canning . . . why does that name sound familiar?' John asked.

'You must have read about it in the papers,' the sexton said. 'His son, who was only nine or ten, managed to get in the way of the police while they were chasing a crime suspect, and the boy was struck by a constable's bullet and died. The Lord works in mysterious ways, to be sure, and many times we cannot understand them. But Mr. Canning was completely inconsolable. Such a pity.'

'John!' I cried. 'Earlier tonight you asked who could hate the police enough to want to eradicate them. It must be he!' Leaving the constable behind, we dashed back to the inspector, who protested our continued presence until we were able to fill him in on our suspicions. He agreed that it all fit together, but was at a loss as to how to get the man out.

'Perhaps if we went ahead and stormed the church, we could subdue him,' Inspector Laurie pondered.

'At the expense of your lives,' I said. 'No, Inspector, the person who enters that church cannot be a policeman.'

'I will go,' the sexton said. 'He is, after all, one of the flock, no matter how far he has strayed.'

'I will go, too,' I declared.

'You most certainly will not!' John

roared. 'It is out of the question!'

'Darling, as a woman I might be able to play upon the man's sympathies.'

'Or you might get yourself blown to bits!' he rejoined. 'I will not permit you to take the chance.'

I turned to the sexton. 'Any explosives would have to be hidden, and most likely they would be in the cellar.'

'There is no cellar here, not as such,' he answered. 'There is only the crypt.'

'You, of course, know how to get there.'

'Of course.'

'Then let us go,' I said, taking his arm and running him as fast as his legs would move to the steps of the church. Behind me I could hear John shouting at me to stop, but I had no intention of doing so, and soon we were inside. 'This way,' the sexton said, grabbing a candle from a stand and leading me through a carefully-disguised door at the back of the nave and down to the dank, musty-smelling crypt below. In the dim light I could make out a few ancient grave markers and some statuary figures placed here and there. It was not a place that I could describe as pleasant. The death-like quiet was suddenly shattered by a voice calling out from the darkness: 'Who is there?'

'We are not the police, Mr. Canning,' I replied.

'Who are you, then? And how do you know me?'

'I am Arthur Dindal, the sexton of St. Mary's,' my companion called out. 'We are here to help you.'

'Where are the police?' the voice demanded. It was coming from the furthest corner of the crypt, which was still obscured by darkness. Taking the candle from Mr. Dindal, I began walking slowly into the shadows, towards the voice.

'They are outside,' I said, 'all of them. There is no need to detonate whatever device you have, Mr. Canning. It would be in vain. The only people you would kill are this servant of God and me. That is not what your son would have wanted.'

'What do you know of my son?'

I continued inching forward with the light until I could barely make out the figure of a man standing over what appeared to be a dozen or so sticks of dynamite bound together by rope. The man himself appeared to be no more than forty years of age, though so savagely careworn and miserable that my heart ached with pity to look upon him. Upon seeing me, he quickly struck a match, then reached down to pick up the end of a long fuse. 'Stay where you are,' he ordered.

I stopped moving. 'Mr. Canning, please tell me about your son,' I said, hoping to occupy him and turn his mind away from his deadly goal.

The man's shoulders slumped. 'Robin was a good boy, the best,' he said quietly. 'He was all I had left, after the death of my wife. I loved watching him grow. I loved listening to him sing. He loved to sing that nursery rhyme.'

I could guess which one he meant.

'I spent all my time with him, and lost my work situation because of it, but I did not mind. Robin was already a better man than anyone in my office. But what did his goodness get him?'

'His death was God's will, Mr.

Canning,' the sexton said.

'God's will, was it?' he suddenly snarled, throwing the burnt match in our direction. 'His own son wasn't enough of a sacrifice? He had to take mine as well?' As the sexton gasped, Mr. Canning added: 'A truly loving God would not have allowed my son to be murdered by the police.'

'Cannot you accept that his death was an accident?' I challenged.

'I cannot. It was murder.'

'And what of the deaths of those beggars by your hand? Were they not murder as well?'

'Those wretches had nothing to live for,' he said solemnly. 'My son had everything to live for.'

'You cannot make such judgment about life and death!' the sexton cried. 'You are not the Almighty!'

'Be quiet, or you will incite him further,' I whispered to the sexton. Then, taking a deep breath, I called out: 'Please, Mr. Canning, come out with us. It is too late to achieve the vengeance you desire. If you light that fuse, you will not hurt the police, you will only hurt your son.'

'How so?' he asked.

'Do you want Robin's memory to be forever linked with the deaths of innocent people and the destruction of this church?'

There was only silence from the man, a silence that was soon rent by a voice shouting from behind us: 'Amelia! Where are you?'

'Who is that?' Mr. Canning said tensely.

'It is my husband,' I said, 'and he is not a policeman either. He is a doctor.'

John then stumbled upon us and quickly took in the situation, then pulled his service revolver from his pocket. 'You, sir!' he barked to Mr. Canning. 'Come away from there. I have a gun, and I am not afraid to use it.'

'John, stay back, please!' I cried.

Mr. Canning merely looked up with an expression of utter defeat and said, 'Then be so good as to shoot, sir. Do me the favour of killing me so that I can be with my son. The woman is right. I can do nothing here. I should be with Robin, taking care of him.'

John lowered the revolver. 'I will not kill you in cold blood.'

'More's the pity,' the man sighed, dropping the fuse. Then, pulling a pistol of his own from his coat, he shouted: 'I am coming, Robin!'

'*No!*' I cried, but it was too late. Before any of us could do anything, he put the pistol to his temple and fired.

'Dear God in heaven,' John muttered, as I turned away.

'May He be merciful,' the sexton said, sadly, and it was all I could do to choke out an 'Amen.'

For the next several days, the newspapers were filled with reports of the Chopper's dramatic detection and demise. Inspector Laurie was touted as a hero and certain to make Chief Inspector before long, and even though we were both included in the letter of thanks from Sir Melville Macnaghten, I insisted that John alone be heralded by the press as having helped to solve the murders and avert disaster at the church. Letting him bask in the attention on his own I hoped would make up for my earlier instance of insensitivity, though obviously I could not explain that to him, which was why he continued to puzzle over my sudden bashfulness.

'Really, Amelia, I do not understand why you think nothing of rushing headlong into physical danger, but then react with dread at the thought of being publicly recognised as the intellect behind the crime's solution,' he told me.

'I had enough of the spotlight when I was young and working on the stage,' I replied. 'I do not wish it now. However, if you feel that strongly that my efforts should be celebrated, why don't you write one of your stories for *The Fleet* magazine about me?' I smiled sweetly, knowing that throughout all of John's writing, he had never once mentioned me; not my name, not even my very existence.

'Hmmm . . . an interesting idea. It would make quite a story.' Immediately he went to his writing desk and picked up his pen and began scratching. After a few minutes he looked up and said, 'However, writing about one's own wife is not going to be easy. You know, Amelia, if you genuinely do not care dear about the publicity, why don't I take your exploits and attribute them to Holmes?'

I have to confess that his suggestion stunned me. 'John, you wouldn't.'

'Why not? Let's see, from who should the information about the nursery rhyme come? We had no girlish maid at Baker Street . . . Ah! Billy, of course! The young street urchin Holmes used as a page. He could have known it. Now, then, dear, would you mind reciting that rhyme for me again?'

Was I now to be replaced in every aspect of my husband's life by Sherlock Holmes? I glared at him, too outraged to speak.

'Dear me, have I said something to offend you?' he asked, guilelessly. But a moment later his innocent expression gave way to a sly smile, and ultimately to a hearty chuckle. Only then did I realise that he was perpetrating a wicked joke at my expense! 'Oh, Amelia, you should see your face!' he laughed, setting down his pen.

Honestly! Of all the times for John to develop a sense of humour!

I joined in the laughter. '*Touché, darling,*' I said. I could afford to permit him his rare joke. I could withstand his jocularity at my expense. I could endure his belief that he had for once and for all bested me. I could do all of that because deep down inside I held the firm conviction that someday, someplace, at some time, I would get even.

The Adventure of the Queen's Letters

There was no question I was being followed. I had already noticed the dark, nondescript brougham staying behind me as I walked down Welbeck Street, never increasing speed, never slowing. As I crossed to Wigmore Street, heading in the direction of Cavendish Square, it turned with me. More annoyed than fearful — it was, after all, an unusually bright and sunny day for late October, hardly the setting for an open-air abduction — I decided to stop and confront my pursuer.

As I approached the brougham, a familiar face emerged from the window. 'Good day, Mrs. Watson,' said Mycroft Holmes, 'I knew I could count on you to detect my presence.'

'You are rather difficult to overlook, Mr. Holmes,' I replied. Mycroft Holmes, the elder brother of my husband's friend Sherlock Holmes, was a man of such size, girth and bearing as to block out the sun on a midsummer day. 'May I ask the reason for this pursuit?'

'A mutual friend requests audience with you on a matter of importance.'

'A mutual friend . . . oh, dear.' There could only be one person Mycroft was referring to, and my pulse quickened at the very thought of an audience with him. 'I take it I am to come with you now?'

'Yes, if it is convenient.'

'And if it is not?' I asked, weakly, but Mycroft had already opened the door of the cab for me to step in. I knew that convenience was not really an issue in a Royal summons.

'I trust Dr. Watson is well,' Mycroft said, after I had settled inside the brougham.

'He is fine, though he is away from home again,' I replied. 'He is visiting an ill friend, someone from his days in the army.'

Mycroft Holmes' face betrayed the slightest touch of a smile. 'I am happy to report that he will find Major Woodbridge much improved — so much so, in fact, that I should think they will have an opportunity to get in some excellent fishing before Dr. Watson is compelled to return to London.'

I glared at him, dumbstruck by his audacity. When I finally spoke, it was to say: 'Have you also arranged for the exact fish he is going to catch? Do you have any idea, Mr. Holmes, what it feels like to be human chess pieces?'

'My sincere apologies, madam, but it was necessary to place your husband out of the way until your business with his majesty is concluded.'

'Exactly why am I being taken to see his majesty?'

'All will be explained,' he assured me, then fell silent, his eyes closed as though asleep, an annoying habit that was shared by his brother Sherlock. This would not be the first time I had been in the presence of his majesty. John and I had previously become involved in a deadly adventure involving the King and, both Holmes brothers, and a German spy disguised as French courtesan. It was my opinion that we had both been rather badly used in that affair, and I had a terrible feeling that history was about to repeat itself.

We arrived at the Buckingham Gate some twenty minutes later and disembarked at the west wing of the Palace, where Mycroft and I were ushered in by a brigade of liveried servants. Striding through the massive (and, to me, intimidating) halls, we eventually stopped in front of a heavy panelled door, upon which Mycroft knocked.

'Ya,' a voice behind the door shouted, and we entered. His Royal Highness King Edward VII was seated comfortably in an overstuffed chair.

'Your majesty,' I said nervously, curtseying before him.

'Rise, Mrs. Watson, rise,' he said, a smile bristling through his beard. 'It is a pleasure to see you again.'

'And you, your majesty. How can I be of service to you?'

'Explain, Holmes,' the King said, then went back to puffing on a cigar.

After directing me to sit down in a chair opposite his majesty, Mycroft then reached into a valise and withdrew a letter. 'Quite recently,' he began, 'the Palace received a communiqué from a man living in the Scottish Highlands, a certain Alexander Brown, who claims to be a nephew of John Brown. You do recall the name John Brown, I trust?'

Even though it had been a good twenty years since the man's death, I did indeed recall the name John Brown, as would have just about anyone else in England who was of a comparable age. A Highlander by birth, John Brown had been a dedicated servant and friend to Queen Victoria in the years after the death of the Prince Consort; and, if one believed the common rumours of the time, more than just a friend. Many thought the servant had an unhealthy influence over the Queen, whom disrespectful gossips had dubbed 'Mrs. Brown'. Carefully phrasing my response, I said: 'I recall the name, yes.'

'A rather delicate matter regarding Mr. Brown and her majesty the Queen, God rest her soul, has come to the attention of the palace,' Mycroft went on. 'This relative of Brown's claims to have uncovered a small cache of private letters between him and her majesty, dating back to the 1870s. These letters, so the man claims, paint a, shall we say, rather intimate relationship between the servant and his Queen.'

'To be blunt,' the King chimed in, 'the blackguard says they are love letters.'

'Just so,' Mycroft went on, 'and he is offering them to the Crown for sale at a rather extreme price. While the missive sent by this Andrew Brown did not contain the word 'blackmail', that may reasonably be inferred. And his majesty detests blackmail.'

I nodded my head, not knowing what else to do.

'Now then, Mrs. Watson, you are no doubt wondering why you have been made privy to this,' Mycroft said, and I nodded once more. 'It is imperative that these letters be examined, yet finding the exact right person to do so has given us some pause. Until, that is, his majesty recommended you.'

'*Me?*' I cried.

'Ya!' the King proclaimed. 'We are not unappreciative of the ways you have helped us in the past, and remained discreet afterwards.'

'Thank you, your majesty,' I stammered, 'but wouldn't you be better served by Mr. Holmes here?'

'In other matters, perhaps,' the King replied. 'But this requires the eye and heart of a woman. You must read these letters, read through the lines on paper, and determine what was in Mama's heart when she wrote them.'

I swallowed hard before speaking. 'So you are convinced these are indeed the letters of the Queen, and not forgeries?'

'We have no doubt that they are authentic,' his majesty said, gravely. 'The questions that must be answered relate to their nature. Let there be no misunderstanding, Mrs. Watson, I did not like Brown. He was an insufferable, vulgar, Highland drunkard who connived his way into the palace to the detriment of all concerned. But Mama would brook no discussion regarding the man's true character, least of all from me.' He paused to regard the glowing ash of his cigar, seeming transfixed by it. 'Now Mama is dead and I am King,' he went on, 'and whatever passed between us is history. As sovereign of the Empire, I will not tolerate any scandal attached to her name, least of all any scandal connected to her Highland gillie. What you must do for us, Mrs. Watson, is examine these letters and determine whether they contain enough scandal to unsettle the foundations of an empire. If so, we have no recourse but to pay the man and retrieve the letters.'

The mood had soured for pleasantries, so after receiving some instruction on how I was to present myself to the bearer of the Queen's letters, I was escorted out of Buckingham Palace and transported back home, feeling quite numb. It was a sensation that remained two days later as, after a painfully long train journey, I stepped out of the Highland chill and into a cramped inn called the Running Man located at the edge of Caithness,

Scotland, a tiny village settled in the shadow of the Grampian Mountains. What few bags I had were being carried by my palace-imposed travelling companion, Lieutenant Benjamin Breakstone, the King's dashing young equerry, whom I had first encountered in my previous adventure with his majesty.

As a travelling companion, I had no complaints about the young soldier, who had forsaken his military uniform in favour of a simple sporting suit and fore-and-aft cap. We chatted easily on the train and with great relish he told me of his family's history in the service of the Crown. His grandfather had been a stable groom for King William IV, and his father, after serving in India, had worked as a palace servant until his death. Benjamin's loyalty to the current sovereign was such that he had requested to accompany me on this peculiar journey. Still, I could not fight down the feeling that he had been ordered along less for my convenience than to keep watch on what I did or said.

After inspecting my room — which was

clean, if only slightly larger than a baking oven — Benjamin and I set out on foot to find the cottage of our contact, Mr. Alexander Brown. The wind had turned biting, so much so that as we came to a quaint footbridge over a brook, I half-expected to see ice in the water.

'Why couldn't this fellow and his letters simply be brought to London?' I asked, holding the collar of my squirrel coat closed against the wind which was equally determined to penetrate it.

'That would make his majesty appear more interested in this matter than he genuinely is,' Benjamin answered.

It seemed to me that his majesty was already vitally interested in this matter, though I said nothing. After a moment, Benjamin pointed to one of a row of cottages that lie ahead of us. 'I believe that is it, Amelia,' he said (for purposes of ease, we had agreed to call ourselves by our Christian names). 'The innkeeper mentioned a gate in front.' Since the smoke that was billowing out of the cottage's chimney promised a welcoming fire, I suggested we make haste. As we neared the cottage, a short, wiry man with a pinched face and thin red hair appeared.

'I'm Brown,' he announced, 'cousin to the late servant o' the queen. Are you they who I'm expecting?'

'We are,' Benjamin announced, and Mr. Brown escorted us inside. The home of Alexander Brown and his wife Jenny, a woman as thin and pinched as he, was quite austere. There were a few furnishings, chiefly a heavy wooden table and some very old chairs, but virtually nothing in the way of decoration on the stark white walls. It was, however, comfortably warm.

'Some tea?' Mrs. Brown asked, and Benjamin and I both nodded, after which she scurried away to the kitchen.

'You'll be wantin' to see the letters,' Mr. Brown said, cutting straight to the matter. Reaching into his coarsely-woven shirt, he withdrew a packet of some twenty envelopes and handed them to Benjamin. 'Well worth a thousand pounds, I would think,' he commented, and from the looks of his home, he could have used the money.

Carefully, Benjamin untied the envelopes and opened one, pulling out a single sheet of paper, which he smoothed out on the table top. From his coat pocket he withdrew a second letter and set it beside the first.

'Wha's that?' Mr. Brown asked.

'A sample of her majesty the Queen's handwriting,' Benjamin replied, 'for comparison purposes.' He scanned back and forth between the two letters. 'The handwriting in your letter, sir, does appear to be genuine.'

Mr. Brown bristled. 'Certain 'tis genuine!' he cried — at least I believe that is what he cried, since it sounded more like, *Sayrre-tin tiss jen-yeuoon*. Mrs. Brown chose that moment to come back with the tea, which proved to be black and very strong.

In another envelope was a letter from John Brown, which Benjamin similarly examined against a sample of handwriting that had been provided by the palace. 'No question,' the equerry said, softly, 'this is Brown's handwriting.'

'*Mister* Brown, if you please,' the dour cottager snapped. 'Woulda been *Sir John* Brown, but for that family o' the queen's.'

'Take care, sir,' Benjamin snapped back. 'We are representatives of the Crown, whose indulgence in this matter can be as easily withdrawn as it was bestowed.'

'Is there a room where we might be allowed to examine these a bit more privately?' I jumped in, hoping to separate the two men.

'I suppose ye could go t' the kitchen,' Mrs. Brown said. 'It's not large, but a goodly light comes through.'

I nodded my thanks and hastened to the kitchen with Benjamin. Even though we would remain within earshot of the glum couple, at least I would not have Andrew Brown peering over our shoulders as we read.

The letters had already been arranged in date order, making them easy to follow. The Queen's letters tended to be small notes of thanks to Brown for carrying out such normal duties as accompanying her on a ride or mediating a dispute among stable grooms. While Her Majesty was clearly taken with her Highland gillie, and given to moments of effusiveness in her praise of him, there was nothing at risk of toppling an empire. For his part, the servant's replies were rather effusive statements of gratitude for the chance to work for her majesty. But in letter after letter, nothing I read could have been construed as scandalous. Nothing, that is, until I came to a letter from Brown dated August 14th, 1879, that had the word *Personal for her majesty* scrawled across the envelope in large block letters. Opening it, I read:

Your Majesty:
As you have requested, I am taking care that other members of the household, particularly your family, do not discover my secret visits to your Royal person. But I have looked into the matter we spoke of in your bedroom the other night —

Oh dear!

— including having words with the

physician, but have not received a satisfactory answer from him. I cannot deny that the offending member in question has failed us both, but that is no reflection on the performance of your Royal self.

I set the letter down and tried to control the flush that was coming into my face. One did not have to be from the lower classes to understand the way in which the word *member* could be used.

'What have you found?' Benjamin asked.

'I cannot yet say, although . . . ' My voice trailed off as I began reading anew:

> *I beg your gracious majesty to be patient with me as I continue to seek an answer, and if it be the answer I suspect, let me put an end to it. If the stone indeed be broken, it shall be by my own hand.*

I did not understand the last line, though before I had an opportunity to contemplate it further, Benjamin asked, 'May I read it?' I handed to him the letter, which he read in silence, frowning, and afterwards folded and placed back in its envelope. 'The implication is certainly unsavoury,' he finally muttered.

'And it is the implication that unnerves me, since that is all that is required for a scandal,' I whispered, hoping not to be overheard. 'I am afraid that this letter alone warrants the payment Mr. Brown is asking. Are you prepared to make such a transaction on behalf of his majesty?'

'I am authorised to do so, yes,' he whispered back, 'but it galls me, Amelia.'

'It galls me too, Benjamin, but consider the alternative.'

He rose and began pacing the small room in an agitated manner, cueing Mr. Brown's appearance in the doorway. 'Are ye t'be much longer, then?' the cottager asked.

'A bit,' I replied, and the man disappeared once more. 'Please sit down, Benjamin. Even if we believe the letter to be incriminating, we must not act as though we are worried. That would encourage them to seek a higher price.

Besides, we are getting ahead of ourselves. There is a letter of reply from the
queen which I have not yet perused.
Perhaps we will learn that the Brown
letter has an innocent meaning.'

The equerry heeded my entreaty and
sat down, though the rhythmic clenching
and unclenching of his fists still demon-
strated that his anger had not yet abated.
I pulled from its envelope the next letter
in the stack, which was dated one day
after Brown's missive.

My dear Brown,
We pray you are in error, though
you so seldom are that you have
unleashed our deepest fears. This
morning we consulted with Bar-
rington and are awaiting his
confirmation. We will do everything
we can to keep this horrid
development away from the eyes
and ears of the household, and trust
you shall do the same.

As I refolded this letter I pondered that,
while not as rife with implication as

Brown's letter, it acknowledged some kind of subterfuge involving the Queen and her gillie. I quickly opened the next letter, which was from Brown.

> *Your Majesty:*
> *All is as we feared. There is nothing left to do but remove the offending member before greater damage to your majesty can be done. As I promised your Royal majesty, I will not seek out the physician, but will do it myself.*

I gasped, as images I care not to reveal flooded my mind. Personally, I wished to read no more, and was sorry for having undertaken this task, but duty to one's King was not to be shirked, so I stuffed the letter back in its envelope and went on to the next one, a reply from the Queen. It was a short note that appeared to have been scrawled in a hurry, but I was able to make out: *Barrington has forwarded us details personally. He will remain silent regarding this matter. Oh, Brown, how we wish this affair had come to a happier conclusion.* Who, I wondered, was Barrington?

That hardly mattered, though, given the contents of the letters. 'I have no alternative but to recommend that you pay the man's price for these,' I told Benjamin, 'after which I wish to return to the inn. I feel like I could use a sherry.'

'Very well,' he replied, and called Mr. Brown into the kitchen. While I neatly sorted the letters in a stack, Benjamin produced a document that stated a series of letters were being purchased on behalf of the Crown for the express purpose of being housed in the Royal Archives, and told the cottager to sign it.

'For the archives,' Mr. Brown sneered as he affixed his name to the document, 'verra clever.' The grating sound that came out of his mouth next might have been a laugh. For a moment, I was worried that the man's sneering attitude was going to further ignite Benjamin's temper, but he remained grimly calm and he reached into his pocket and withdrew a roll of bank notes, counting off a thousand pounds' worth and laying them on the table. Mrs. Brown now joined us, and at the sight of the money, her eyes enlarged to the size of full moons. 'Och, Sandy . . . ' was all she uttered. With the letters safely tucked inside Benjamin's coat, we hastily took leave of the Browns, and despite the cold, it felt good to be outside once again.

'What will happen to the letters now?' I asked as we made our way back to the inn.

'That is for his majesty to decide,' he answered tersely. Clearly, this entire affair was still upsetting him.

The rest of that day was uneventful, as was our modest dinner, which was taken in the public room of the Running Man. But before I retired for the evening, I asked Benjamin if I could once more examine the letters.

'You are not having second thoughts about purchasing them, I hope,' he said.

'No, not at all, it is simply that his majesty requested that I read between the lines of the letters, so to speak, in hopes of discerning what was in the Queen's heart when she wrote them. I have to admit that upon reading them in the cottage I concentrated only on their surface meanings. I should merely like to examine them again with a more open mind.' That was the truth, at least in part. What I did not tell him was that there was some niggling little question concerning the letters sticking in the back of my mind, something that I could not bring forth.

'Very well,' he said, taking the envelopes from his pocket. 'Please let nothing happen to them.'

'I promise,' I said. 'Good night.' I retreated to my room and he to his. Once inside, I set a lamp close and re-examined the notes, attempting to peer underneath the words, searching for any possible hidden meaning. Even given Brown's legendary bluntness, it was hard to imagine he would write in such coarse fashion to his sovereign.

But upon re-reading the letter for what must have been the tenth time, I finally found what I was looking for. Brown had used the word *member* in two different contexts. I read again: *I am taking care that other members of the household, particularly your family, do not discover my secret visits to your Royal person.*

Other members of the household . . . *member* . . . I quickly scanned the lines again: *the member in question has failed us both . . . remove the offending member* . . . 'Oh, good heavens!' I moaned. 'Not two different contexts, but one.' I had stupidly fallen into the trap of succumbing to suggestion, seeing evidence of a scandal simply because I had been predisposed to see it. But the letters could be read with an entirely different meaning: *member* could refer to a member of the household staff. In that context, *failed us both* implied the person serving the Queen was not performing his or her duties as prescribed by Brown, while *removing* implied that they were dismissed as a result, an unenviable task that was taken on by John Brown personally to spare the Queen any further trouble. She had asked him to investigate, just as the King had asked me to investigate, and as for Brown's being in the Queen's bedroom, that must have been for reasons of secrecy. After all, hadn't I once found myself in the King's bedchamber?

'What a fool I've been,' I muttered aloud. Just as I had been commissioned by his royal majesty to undertake this delicate assignment, so had the King's mother, Queen Victoria, entrusted her servant to resolve a delicate matter involving a problem in the household. As I re-read the final letter from the Queen, I did indeed see through the words and into her heart. *How we wish this affair had come to a happier conclusion*, she wrote, genuinely regretful that someone in the palace household had been made redundant, perhaps because a medical condition had been involved, hence the references to a physician.

Now it all made sense . . . almost. There was still the mysterious Barrington, and Brown's cryptic phrase *stone indeed be broken*, though perhaps that was simply a Highland expression of which I was unfamiliar. What was interesting was that if one reversed the first and last words . . . 'Oh, good heavens!' I cried, placing a hand on my forehead. Could it really be?

Tucking the letters back in their envelopes, I quickly donned my coat and dashed out of my room, only to find Benjamin in the hallway. 'Did you find what you were seeking?' he asked.

'I cannot be sure,' I replied, returning the envelopes to him. 'I fear I have overtaxed my brain. I need to step out for a bit of fresh air. My room is a bit stifling.'

'Shall I accompany you?'

'No, thank you, I prefer to go alone,' I told him. 'I won't be long.' As casually as I could, I made my way down to the public house, then quietly asked the innkeeper's wife where I might find a telephone. 'The constable has the only one in the village,' she replied, giving me directions. It was quick walk to the constable's station (made all the longer by having to walk against the stinging cold wind), and it took a few minutes to convince the small, red-faced constable of Caithness to allow me to use the device. I requested the London exchange and gave the number of Mycroft Holmes's office in Whitehall, praying that he would still be there. It rang for five seconds before a familiar voice answered, 'Holmes.'

'Mr. Holmes, it's Amelia Watson,' I said.

There was a pause before he replied. 'Indeed? I did not expect to receive a telephone call from you. Is there a problem?'

'Not exactly. I'm just, well, I've come across a bit of a puzzle.'

'And you will not be able to rest until you have satisfied yourself regarding it.'

'Something like that,' I acknowledged. 'In the letters from the Queen, there was a reference to someone named Barrington. Do you know who that could be?'

'Sir William Macaulay Barrington, the Royal Physician, I should think,' he answered, which made perfect sense. Brown's 'physician' and the Queen's 'Barrington' were one and the same, but what had he to do with the unfortunate staff member's dismissal?

'As long as I am speaking with you,

madam, may I inform his majesty that he may rest assured these letters will be causing the Crown no further problem?'

'We are bringing the letters with us, Mr. Holmes, and while at first glance their content does indeed appear distressing, I believe I have discovered their correct interpretation, which is far more innocent.'

'I shall see you upon your return to London, then,' he said, and the line then went dead.

I slept fitfully that night, unable to switch off my mind as it tried to correctly assemble the puzzle pieces that made up the affair of the Queen's letters. Arising early to catch the day's first train back to London made me feel rushed and exhausted. I would have time to rest, of course, over the course of the journey, though there was something I had to do first.

'I am somewhat surprised, Lieutenant Breakstone, that you have not yet asked me what I discovered regarding those letters,' I told him, once we had settled into the train compartment.

'I assumed that you would save your report for his majesty,' he responded.

'Would it be too much trouble to see them again?'

'Whatever for?'

'To satisfy one last bit of curiosity.'

Hesitantly, he pulled the packet of envelopes from his pocket and handed them to me. As I had anticipated, one was now missing.

'All of them, Benjamin, or have you destroyed the most damaging one already?'

'Whatever do you mean?'

'It is no longer necessary to pretend,' I said. 'I know what the letters are really about.'

All soldierly demeanour ebbed away and Benjamin appeared to be fighting back tears as he withdrew a solitary envelope from the inside breast pocket of his jacket. A quick glance at the letter confirmed that it was the one containing the odd reference, *stone indeed be broken*, a play on the name *Breakstone*. 'Tell me about your father, Benjamin.'

'He was a fine man and a loyal servant,'

he replied, 'but he had a problem.'

'Drink?' I ventured.

Benjamin shook his head. 'Opium. He picked the habit up while he was stationed in the East. Years after his death, my mum told me that he had been discovered stealing the stuff from the medical bag of the Royal Physician.'

'Dr. Barrington.'

'I was only seven years old when it happened, Amelia, and I didn't know anything about opium or any other kind of drug. All I knew was that my father was sacked by that damned Highland gillie, and it crushed him.'

'But it was done at the request of the Queen herself.'

'No,' Benjamin cried. 'Brown was only told to investigate the matter and report back to her majesty. Giving Father the sack was his own idea. Even these letters prove that.'

I suddenly realised why Benjamin had become so agitated yesterday at the cottage of Alexander Brown. It had nothing to do with insult to the Royal family or the thought of blackmail against the Crown. It was instead the anger of a loyal son wanting to defend the memory of his father.

'I know Father wasn't perfect,' he went on, 'but I promise you that if he had been a Scot and his problem *had* been drink, an affliction close to Brown's own heart, he would have been given another chance and he might still be alive today.'

'What do you mean?'

Benjamin looked up at me with red-rimmed eyes. 'Father could not take the disgrace of being found out. He shot himself.'

The words, *Oh, Brown, how we wish this affair had come to a happier conclusion* echoed in my mind. 'Benjamin, I am so sorry.'

'Ever since her majesty's death I have endeavoured to involve myself in any matter that concerns John Brown, in hopes I can eradicate his name from public memory.'

'That is why you volunteered to accompany me.'

He nodded. 'Now I suppose you will tell all this to Mycroft Holmes.'

'I would be very much surprised if Mr. Holmes did not already know, since he seems to know everything else,' I replied. 'On the chance that he does not, however, he will not learn it from me.' I got up to pull down the compartment shades. 'Do you have a match on you?'

Looking somewhat puzzled, Benjamin withdrew a match from his vest pocket.

'Strike it,' I said, and he did so. Then I held the incriminating letter to the flame and we watched as the paper seared and withered into ash. I handed the rest of the envelopes back to Benjamin. 'The Queen asked Brown to investigate a matter of personnel,' I said. 'He did so, secretly detecting and dismissing a member of the Palace staff. It is all contained in these letters, except for the identity of the servant, which we will never know.'

'Thank you, Amelia,' Benjamin sighed. 'If there is ever anything I can do for you in return, just call on me.'

'There is,' I said, 'please wake me when we reach Rugby.' I then leaned my head back and fell fast asleep.

We do hope that you have enjoyed reading this large print book.

Did you know that all of our titles are available for purchase?

We publish a wide range of high quality large print books including:

Romances, Mysteries, Classics
General Fiction
Non Fiction and Westerns

Special interest titles available in large print are:

The Little Oxford Dictionary
Music Book, Song Book
Hymn Book, Service Book

Also available from us courtesy of Oxford University Press:

Young Readers' Dictionary
(large print edition)
Young Readers' Thesaurus
(large print edition)

For further information or a free brochure, please contact us at:
Ulverscroft Large Print Books Ltd.,
The Green, Bradgate Road, Anstey,
Leicester, LE7 7FU, England.
Tel: (00 44) **0116 236 4325**
Fax: (00 44) **0116 234 0205**

Other titles in the
Linford Mystery Library:

DEATH DIMENSION

Denis Hughes

When airline pilot Robert Varden's plane is wrecked in a thunderstorm, he goes to bail out. As he claws his way through the escape hatch, he is struck by lightning and his consciousness fades into oblivion. Miraculously, Varden cheats death, and awakes in hospital after doctors succeed in saving his life. But he emerges into an unfamiliar world that is on the brink of devastating war, and where his friends are mysteriously seventeen years older than he remembered them . . .

MRS. WATSON AND THE DEATH CULT

Michael Mallory

When the body of a prominent businessman is found floating in an ancient Roman bath, all the evidence points to a young man named Ronald Standish as the murderer. His wife appeals to her old governess Amelia, the second wife of Dr. John H. Watson, for help. Soon, Amelia is thrust into a baffling mystery involving the practice of ancient pagan religious rites in the modern city of Bath. At every step, though, she finds evidence that makes the case against Standish even stronger . . .

THE LORD HAVE MERCY

Shelly Smith

The married life of Robert Mansbridge and his wife Editha is the talk of the village. Whispers of infidelity and wantonness abound; whilst most of their neighbours respect the doctor, Editha is regarded as a shrew. Meanwhile, timid Catherine Duncton is hopelessly in love with Robert, but chained to her invalid father; and sculptor Leslie Crispin carries a torch for Editha. Then Editha dies in mysterious circumstances, and the rumour mill churns ever faster and more fiercely . . .

THE NEXT TO DIE

Gerald Verner

When a body is found under a pile of gravel at the foot of a bank, it looks as if the storm the previous night blew a cart-load over just as the man was passing underneath. But amateur criminologist Trevor Lowe notices that the soles of the dead man's shoes are caked with cigarette ash: clearly he never walked to the gravel site, but was carried there. It is the first of a whole series of murders. Can Lowe unmask the criminal — or will he be the next to die?

BLACK BARGAIN

Victor Rousseau

Joan Wentworth, a newly qualified nurse, nearly faints from the ether whilst assisting the famous surgeon, Dr. Lancaster, and is promptly suspended from her job. That evening, when she pleads with him to reinstate her, she is surprised to be invited to work at his hospice that serves the poor hill people of Pennsylvania. Joan accepts; but on her arrival at the remote institute, she finds herself plunged into an atmosphere of menace and mystery. No one there seems to be normal — not least Dr. Lancaster himself when he visits . . .